DEATH OF
INNOCENCE

CHARLES RAY

North Potomac, MD

This book is a work of fiction. Names, descriptions, places, and incidents are products of the author's imagination, or are used fictionally. Any resemblance to actual events or persons, living or dead, is purely coincidental.

For information about this and other works of this author, contact the author at charlesray.author@yahoo.com.

Cover photo by the author

Author photograph by Denise Ray-Wickersham

Printed in the United States of America.

ISBN: 0692694153
ISBN-13: 978-0692694152

Dedication

To everyone who enjoys a good mystery. If you like what
you read, why not leave a review on your blog or favorite
book site?

ONE

Some people don't have to go looking for trouble. All they have to do is sit idle in one place long enough, because trouble is always looking for them, and whether they wish it or not, trouble finds them.

That's me. It describes me perfectly. When I have nothing to do, trouble has a way of sneaking up on my blind side and kicking me in the nuts. My grandmother always used to say that 'idle hands are the devil's main tools.' She could just as well have said that idle people are the devil's main targets.

You'd think by now I'd know better.

It's been that way for as long as I can remember. When I was a kid, when the other kids were enjoying a school break or holiday, I was usually busy getting that bitch, Karma, off my ass. During my time in the army, every time I went on a furlough or R&R I ended up in trouble. The only way I found to stay out of trouble was to stay busy. It didn't do Jack shit for my social life, but it got me promoted pretty fast, so I guess that cloud at least did have a silver lining. Problem is, though, clouds also have a tendency to dump rain on you. A friend of mine in basic training said it was like someone up there was pissing on all us fools stuck down here. The only way to keep from getting pissed on was to keep moving. Well, the only way to keep from getting pissed on too much.

You'd think that after a lifetime of learning that down time was dangerous for me, I'd do anything to avoid it. The problem is, though, avoiding down time in my line of work is hard to do.

I'm a private investigator. Not the kind you see on TV or in the movies. I seldom get involved in toe-to-toe confrontations with bad guys, and I don't do shootouts. In fact, since I left the army nearly two decades ago, I've only used a firearm once, and that was in a situation I'd tried to avoid, but my hand was forced. I'm pretty good in a number of Asian martial arts, and I have a pretty quick wit. If I can't talk my way out of it or smash my way out with fist or foot, I run like hell away from it. There's absolutely nothing wrong with running away if the alternative is getting killed. I don't know who said that, but it works for me.

But, getting back to being a private eye. I'm paid ten grand a month retainer by the law firm of Holcombe, Stein and Chang, where my old army buddy, Quincy Chang is a senior partner. That money buys my services doing the occasional odd job for them; odd in that they come along five or six times a month. They consist of tracking down missing heirs, serving dunning notices to pikers who don't want to pay their legal fees, and doing the occasional background check on prospective clients. Not exactly blood-tingling excitement and I don't even do the background checks. That latter task is assigned to my associate, Heather Bunche. Formerly my secretary, office manager, and assistant, Heather recently got her license in Maryland, Virginia and the District of Columbia—same as me—and is now a full-fledged partner of 'A.E. Pennyback, Confidential Enquiries,' a two-person investigative outfit located on the second floor of a building off Fourth Street in Southwest DC a few blocks north of the historic Fort Lesley J. McNair army base.

Our building looks like one of those fly by night motels you see along the back roads when you travel south. You know the kind with a 'Vacancy' sign with missing bulbs, and an ice machine that never works. The only signs we have are the ones on the various doors, marking the businesses who can't afford more expensive offices in other parts of the city, and we have no ice machine. The heating and air conditioning, with individual controls in each office, work most of the time, and I've yet to see rats in the building—the four-legged variety, that is to say.

I hired Heather right after I let Quincy talk me into starting the business as therapy after my wife, Sara, and son, Ethan, were killed in an auto accident, and I took early retirement from the army and dove into a deep depression. She was fresh from secretarial school and needed a job, and I was still depressed and a disaster at paperwork.

It turned out to be a winning arrangement for both of us. She got a job with a fairly regular salary, and I got someone to keep the place straight. Of course, I got the best of the deal, because, in addition to her office management skills, she has an elaborate network of contacts among the personal assistants and office managers of people around the Washington area, and she's a Svengali when it comes to computers and computer networks. If it's on a computer system—other than the National Security Agency's highly encrypted machines—Heather can figure a way to coax it out. I'm only assuming that, mind you, because there haven't been any goons from NSA paying us a call.

So, that's pretty much what we do. Now and then, a case comes in over the transom that's not ordinary. Actually, almost everything that comes in over the transom has to be called extraordinary—or just odd. Our most recent case involved a man who wanted me to find his wife, who had reportedly been killed in an auto accident and cremated by her father. That one turned into a murder and abuse case that ended badly for my client, but I wouldn't call it exciting. Since then, though, we'd been gliding along, serving the occasional paper, looking up the indiscretions of a client or two, and sitting in the office watching the cobwebs slowly form in the corners of the ceilings and listening to the scurrying of the cockroaches in the walls. Yeah, while we don't have rats—as far as I know—we do have cockroaches. Damned things are likely to be the only life to survive if the earth gets hit by a meteor.

There you have it. We had no cases to work on. Heather could always play with her computer. But, as for me, I was idle. A twitchy little feeling in my lizard brain told me that trouble was just around the corner.

I was at a loss, though. Knowing trouble's coming is not the same as knowing in what form. It's kind of like a mental puzzle, or a diagramless; one of those blank grids with lots of questions, but without a clue as to where the answers fit in the grid, and worse, in my mental state, unlike the blank grids where you always start in the upper left corner, I had no idea where to start filling in the answers. Hell, I wasn't even sure I knew the questions.

So, I did what I always do when I'm sitting in my office with time to kill. I booted up the Hewlett Packard laptop in the center of my desk, and killed some more time watching the colors and shapes swirl around on the screen until it finally settled down and my home screen sat there mindlessly staring back at me. Heather had shown me how to put the little pictures called icons on the screen that represent my most frequently used applications—computer jargon that meant about as much to me as cuneiform on an old vase—that you only had to jiggle the mouse (other than the fact that it was a device that looked like a mouse with its head, tail, and legs amputated, I was at a loss as to why it was called a mouse) until the little arrow was over the icon you wanted, and then you pressed the right button, the button on the left front of the mouse, that is, to open it. Now, I've never understood why they call the darned thing an application and not a program, which was the word I'd learned in the army for the crap on the computer you played or worked with, but, that's what Heather insisted they were called, and she's the computer expert in the company, so who am I to argue.

I put the arrow over the icon that was a picture of a chess piece—the Knight—and clicked the right button—the left button, which is the *correct* one. You see why computers confuse me. They screw up common language so that nothing means what it should mean anymore. There was some more swirling and flashing, and my chess game was finally on the screen.

Heather had loaded—she said downloaded, except I never understood where they came *down* from—several games onto my computer, but chess was my favorite. Not, mind you, because I'm such a good chess player. I'm not bad, but my record against the computer is running something in the neighborhood of twenty losses to one win— and, that's a generous assumption, because the computer usually mates me in less than thirty moves. Chess is my favorite, though, because it's a game that forces you to think, not, like most computer games, just react, or see how fast your fingers can move.

On screen was a fairly accurate two-dimensional representation of a chess board, with the white and black pieces already in place. Beneath the image was a line of type, 'Which Color Do You Wish to Play - White or Black? Choose One.' It blinked annoyingly. I usually played white, which gave me the opening move, but on this day, I decided to see what the computer would do to start the game. I put the arrow on 'White' and clicked the mouse button. The game shimmered for a few seconds, and then the white King's Pawn blinked out and reappeared two squares forward, a notation, 'pK4,' appeared in a box beside the board. I responded in kind, moving my King's Pawn two spaces forward by clicking first on the piece, and then on the square to which I wanted it to move. As soon as my pawn appeared on the desired square, the white King's Knight blinked out and reappeared on King's Bishop 3. I recognized the classic Ruy Lopez opening, and groaned. One of the most popular chess openings, it's damned hard for even the most experienced chess players to defend against, and against a computer that could keep hundreds of thousands, perhaps even millions, of potential moves in memory, I stood about as much chance of winning as a snowball did of rolling through hell without losing weight.

I was bored, but not bored enough to subject myself to the embarrassment and torture. Besides, I know when I'm in over my head. I'm a chess player who likes to hold my Knights in reserve until the middle game, taking advantage of that dogleg move of theirs to spring on my opponent, much like the cavalry was used for in the wars of the nineteenth century. To me, the Lopez strategy, while effective, used them too early, thus squandering their surprise effect. Okay, that's a crock. I just didn't want to lose another game to the computer.

I put the little arrow on 'Quit' and pressed the left button. "Are you sure you want to Quit?" a line of text appeared on the screen superimposed over the chess board. Well, of course I do, or why else would I click on quit. I know this is done to ensure that if someone's selected 'Quit' by mistake they have a chance to correct it, but it always struck me as a bit patronizing. I puffed out a gust of breath and clicked 'Yes,' mumbling, "Take that, you dumb machine." The screen blinked and then went dark, then it blinked again, transforming itself back into what Heather calls my 'home' screen, which is a bright blue background with my little icons stacked neatly in two rows down the left side. For some crazy reason that little routine always amuses me, but then again, I was bored, so it didn't really take much to amuse me.

The picture of an envelope at the top of the left row caught my eye. That one's for my email, which I hadn't checked in a couple of days. Not that it mattered. It's usually nothing but advertising for junk I don't need and would never buy, so every couple of days I open it up and delete everything. That's another thing Heather insists I do to keep things neat. A computer is supposed to make your life easier, but it seems to me, I spend as much time tending to the damn thing to keep it from getting clogged up as I did when there was nothing but paper to deal with. I still get junk mail, which is now called spam. Another thing I don't understand about computers. Why in hell do they call something you don't like spam? Hell, I like spam. There's nothing I like better than a fried spam and peanut butter sandwich, washed down with a cold beer. During the

Korean War, American GIs and starving Koreans survived on the stuff, and it's still considered a delicacy by many Koreans. In Hawaii, you can get it in restaurants.

But, I digress. I was telling you why I don't think of computers as time savers. I still have to wade through page after page of documents, except now those pages are on a tiny screen, and they're tinier, making them harder to read the older I get, and I have to learn to do something called scrolling instead of just flipping a page. In the past, I'd just grab up all the junk mail in a bundle and drop it in the nearest trash bin. Now, I have to delete it item by item. Time saver my ass.

I clicked on the envelope anyway, and as expected, the fifty emails were all solicitations for useless crap, ranging from payday loans to pills to enhance my masculinity. I selected everything in my inbox and clicked on the delete button, and everything disappeared, leaving a blank grid on the screen with the message, 'You have nothing in your inbox.' There it went again. Damn machine telling me what my eyes can plainly see. I think the people who design computer programs must think the rest of us are pretty dumb.

With an empty mailbox and no desire to let the computer trounce me at chess, I was left to stare at the walls, which have nothing but a couple of old hunting prints and a framed and autographed photo of me with Colin Powell when he was Chairman of the

Joint Chiefs of Staff and I was a lieutenant colonel working at the Pentagon, or stare out the lone window in my broom closet of an office. I chose the window. The view's not fantastic, what with the trees in full foliage in early May and the imposing towers of concrete, steel, and glass condominiums forming walls to either side. But, through the tiny gaps in the foliage, I can get little slivers of glimpses of the Washington Channel, with its sailboats, and beyond that, the bluish smudge that's the Potomac River. When I get real bored, I sit there and see if I can get a brief glimpse of planes coming in for landings at National Airport—now named for Ronald Reagan, the B-movie star who became president. I still insist on calling it National Airport, which gets me strange looks the few times I have to take a taxi. It's not that I'm opposed to change, but the guy already had a building in downtown DC named for him. Why the hell did he need an airport too?

That's it. That's what I do between cases. I sit in my office waiting for the trouble that I know will come.

And, come it did. In the most unlikely form. It came in as a five-foot-four, bouncy, blue-eyed, blonde with a beaming smile on her cherubic face.

Heather opened the door and peeked around the frame at me.

"Al, you will not believe who is here in our office," she said in a breathless 'I'm about to hyperventilate and pass out' voice. "I mean, you just *won't* believe it."

TWO

I swiveled around in my chair and gave my partner the best version of a steely-eyed, iron-jawed look that I could manage. My face muscles were so slack from boredom, though, I'm not sure I managed much beyond a slightly constipated expression.

"So, if I won't believe it," I said. "Why even bother. Why don't you just tell me who it is?"

She pouted at me, but the look of excitement didn't leave her eyes. "You're no fun at all," she said.

I tried hard, unsuccessfully, to suppress a laugh, which caused her pout to deepen, and some of the excitement in her eyes faded a fraction. "Okay," I said. "Sorry for being such a grump. I guess I'm just bored, what with nothing to do. Who is here in our office pray tell?"

She wasn't through making me grovel, though.

"Who is the last person you'd expect to be

in this part of town, in *our* offices?"

Okay, I'd play along. I was willing to do almost anything to bring that broad smile back.

"Is it the president?"

"No, silly, the president doesn't use private investigators. At least, I don't think he does." She made fists and slapped them against her thighs. "Oh, you're no fun at all. Jacob Sonnenberg is here in *our* office."

I looked blankly at her.

"You don't know who Jacob Sonnenberg is, do you?" She looked at me as if I'd just said I didn't know who George Washington was.

"Is it that obvious? So, who is Jacob Sonnenberg?"

She blew out a breath and crossed her arms under her breasts. "If you read more, you'd know. Jacob Sonnenberg just happens to be one of the most famous writers in the Washington, DC area."

"Does he write mysteries or military history?" These happen to be the two main genres I read.

"Gr-r-r, no, he writes a wine column for *The Washington Insider.*"

Well, that explained why I didn't know him. I'm not much of a wine drinker, and I'd never heard of the publication. I fought back a smile. "He's a wine writer. Interesting, that is very interesting." Not really. "What does a wine writer for *The Washington Insider* want with us?"

"He wouldn't tell me," she said. "But, he's acting really nervous. Says it's important and he'll only talk to you about it."

"Didn't you tell him you're a full-fledged investigator just like me?"

"Of course I did, but he said *you* were personally recommended, and he'll only talk to you."

"In that case I guess you'd better show him in."

She ducked out and a few seconds later the door swung inward all the way. Jacob Sonnenberg swept into the room. As trite as that sounds, it's the only way I can describe the way the man moved.

He moved like a much bigger man. He was, in fact, a tiny stick of a man, around Heather's height, but probably five pounds lighter. He was so small he looked like a strong wind would blow him away. His tiny body, with its bowed shoulders and sunken chest, was topped by a tiny lemon shaped head sparsely covered by wisps of brown hair combed over in front to cover a growing bald spot. He had that pasty, fish-belly white complexion of someone who doesn't spend much time outdoors, a thin nose that curled downwards a bit at the tip, and thin, colorless lips that looked like a line drawn across beneath his nose. He held his head in a way that, despite his shortness, made it look like he was peering down his nose at you. As he walked through the door, he flicked at the cuff of his expensive, tailor-made blue suit, and then adjusted a red and yellow striped silk tie, before extending a slender, manicured hand toward me, looking as if he'd just as soon I didn't take it.

"Mr. Pennyback, so nice of you to make time to see me," he said, in a faux English accent that I'd heard many easterners use on occasion, and which tended to grate on my ears. "Forgive me for not calling in advance for an appointment, but your friend, Quincy Chang, said I should just . . . how did he put it . . . drop in."

Well, that explained one thing; how he came our way, leaving only the why. I waved him toward the chair beside my desk, the one I keep for the infrequent visitors to my office. "Why don't you bring in one for yourself," I said to Heather. "I hope you don't mind if my partner sits in on this."

He gave me that down the nose look as if I was of no real consequence. "No, not at all," he said as he settled himself on the chair, carefully smoothing the legs of his trousers so that they fell straight with the crease perfectly centered. I'm not crazy about clothes, preferring to buy mine off the rack at Old Navy, but I couldn't help but silently admire his clothing. His suit probably cost more than everything in my closet. I would never have guessed that writing about fermented grape juice could be so lucrative.

Heather was back quickly with one of the three chairs she keeps in what we call our waiting area—the blank wall opposite her desk—which she placed at the right side of my desk. I then sat in the big, scuffed black leather executive chair that I got at a government surplus auction several years ago. It made a squeaking sound as I settled in.

"Okay," I said. "Now, how can we help you?"

He studied his nails for a few seconds before looking at me. When he did, I found his expression confusing. I couldn't tell if it was anger or sadness. That bothered me. I can usually read people easily, but this guy was about as easy to read as the Dead Sea Scrolls.

Finally, he spoke. "My wife is missing," he said.

That brought me up short. We'd just recently handled a missing wife case; it had turned into a murder case. I hate domestic cases. They're messy, and there are seldom any winners. I absolutely refuse to touch cheating spouse cases.

"We don't do missing persons cases," I said.

He held up a hand, as if waving me to silence.

"Oh, you don't understand, this is not your usual missing person case. What I mean, is I don't exactly want you to *find* my wife, although I suppose you might have to do that in order to do what I really want you to do."

Are you confused? I was. I understood every single word of what he said, but had no idea what he meant, and it must have shown on my face.

"I suppose it would be better if I put more fully in the picture," he said. His tone was lecturing, almost hectoring, as if I was some kind of not-too-bright student who was failing to understand a simple equation like $E=MC^2$. The fact that I didn't have a clue is immaterial, you understand. As a potential client, it's his job to be clear about what he's hiring us for. "My wife has been . . . missing for ten days now, since April 28 to be exact."

We'd just done a case involving husband who claimed his wife wasn't dead, just missing. He'd been right, but for the wrong reasons. A little voice in the back of my mind started telling me to wave this one off, but Sonnenberg kept talking.

"It happened when we were visiting the Brandywine Estates out near Warrenton, Virginia," he said. "I was there to taste a new vintage the estate's orchard is planning to launch in the Washington area market. I took my wife Leana along because she'd been complaining about me going off on these assignments and leaving her alone in our place in Georgetown."

On the one hand, that voice was still

saying, 'avoid it,' but another little voice was straining to be heard. That voice was curious as to where this tale was going.

"Your wife went missing in a grape orchard?" I asked.

"Technically it's called a vineyard," he said down his nose at me, still in that lecturing-to-an-idiot tone. "But, yes, that's essentially it."

Now, the curious voice was loudest. "How does one get lost in a . . . vineyard? I mean, aren't the vines planted in rows? All you have to do is walk to the end of a row and you're out of it."

His thin eyebrows arched upwards and he gave me a strange look. I interpreted that to mean he thought I was casting doubt on what he'd said. Ordinarily I wouldn't have given two figs, but my curiosity had hold of me—I wanted to know more. "I do not doubt your story," I said. "I'm just trying to understand how someone could go missing in a place like that."

His brows came down and the muscles in his face relaxed, but his lips remained pursed as if he'd been sucking on a lemon. He gave me another of those 'down the nose' looks. "I take it you're not familiar with viniculture," he said.

It took me a second to process the word; of course, the growing of vines, in this case grape vines. He was right, though. You could take what I know about growing grapes and stick it in your eye and it wouldn't cause any irritation.

"I'm a total blank slate," I said. "Is it possible for someone to get lost in a vineyard?"

He put a finger on his nose and stared up at the ceiling, then back down at me. "That would depend upon the size of the vineyard, and how it was laid out," he said. "And, of course, what lay beyond the vineyard. Some of the vineyards in Virginia border on some pretty rugged terrain."

I was beginning to get a fuzzy picture. "So, if someone followed the rows to the wrong end of the vineyard, they might get lost in the woods?"

The put upon lecturer look came back to his face.

"I suppose if one was disoriented or drunk that could happen," he said. "But, a person with full faculties would only, upon encountering the fence and the woods beyond, have to reverse course and they would be back inside the vineyard proper."

Well, of course. I would have thought of that.

"Okay, we've established that I don't know jack about vineyards, so why don't you tell me how your wife turned up missing."

"Ah, yes," he said. "I'm not at all certain. Perhaps if I start at the beginning you'll understand."

He and his wife had, according to his

account, arrived at Brandywine Estates and gone directly to the suite that had been reserved for them. They arrived around three in the afternoon, and his plan had been to relax in the room until a planned dinner and wine tasting event scheduled for 7:00. But, Leana—he pronounced the name, LEE-ANNA, with stress on the middle syllable—had wanted to accept the manager's invitation to tour the vineyards with some of the other guests. He'd argued against it, but she was insistent, and they'd argued briefly until he finally threw his arms up in resignation and told her to enjoy her romp in the afternoon sun with the dust and commoners. She'd fired back a few choice expletives, and gone off in a huff with the manager to join the group, while he took a shower and a nap, waking up at 6:00 and beginning to dress for the evening event. He'd expected her to be back by the time he'd finished his nap, but by 6:40 she still hadn't returned. Concerned, he sought out the manager, who informed him that he'd been told by one of the vineyard workers that Mrs. Sonnenberg had changed her mind before the tour started and had gone off to explore the estate's sculptured English gardens, and he hadn't seen her since. When Sonnenberg informed him rather pointedly that she hadn't returned to the room, the manager called the groundskeeper and had him and three laborers check the gardens and vineyards, but there was no sign of her. She had, he said, disappeared into thin air.

"I'm assuming that you called the police at this point?"

"Yes, the manager called the Fauquier County Sheriff's Department," he said. "They sent a two deputies out, and they talked to everyone there, and walked back over the same ground that the workers had already searched. There wasn't a trace of her anywhere."

This was beginning to sound interesting. People don't just vanish without a trace, and I don't care what the alien abduction freaks say, they don't get snatched up by aliens to be taken to a spaceship for probing. I'd been sitting morosely in my office pining for something to sink my teeth into, and this foppish old man had dished up a veritable feast.

"We don't normally do missing persons," I said, which wasn't precisely the truth. "But, we'll take yours."

THREE

Jacob Sonnenberg was not the client who usually came in over the transom. They tended for the most part to be lower middle class, people just getting by on meager pay from dull jobs, or people with something they didn't want to share with the authorities, like our last client who wanted us to find his wife so he could kill her. Sonnenberg was clearly not someone who was *just* getting by.

When I told him that our fee was five hundred a day plus expenses, and we'd need a thousand dollar deposit, he didn't even bat an eye. He just took out a leather-bound checkbook and a black Montblanc Meisterstuck pen with pearl inlaid, and wrote a thousand check as blithely as I swipe my credit card for a tank of gas.

And, despite the fact that his manner rubbed me the wrong way, most rich people do, I didn't get the feeling that he was hiding anything. There were none of the indicators of evasion or deceit that people with something to hide usually display.

The final hook, though, was that this represented a puzzle, and I am unable to resist a puzzle. I'm like the character who answers a pay phone because he cannot *not* answer a phone.

While Heather went back to her desk to type up a contract, I pulled a notebook from my desk drawer, along with a Paper Mate pen that Heather had bought in bulk from Office Depot, and began the process of getting the details from him to help construct a framework from which to begin the process of investigating the case.

"Let's start with details about your wife," I said.

"What kind of details?" he asked.

"Everything you can think of, starting with her date of birth, a full description, favorite credit cards, friends, family; things I need to map out a search."

He was hesitant at first, but I convinced him that I would seriously search for his wife, and I'd need to know as much as possible about her if I was have any hope of tracking her down. As he finally began to give me the information, I wrote it all down in my notebook.

Leana Sonnenberg, nee Colman, thirty-seven years old, was, surprisingly, a military veteran. She'd served for ten years in the U.S. Army as a truck driver from the time she was nineteen until just after her twenty-ninth birthday. Except for a three-year tour in Germany, and two weeks driving a supply truck out of Kuwait City after it was liberated at the tail-end of the first Gulf War, she'd spent her time in the U.S., mainly at Fort Belvoir, Virginia and Fort Meade, Maryland. Sonnenberg couldn't tell me why she left the military after serving half the time needed to be eligible for full retirement, only that he'd met her at a wine tasting in Baltimore where she was living and working as a part time truck driver while getting her degree in art history at Towson State University. "She never liked to talk about her last few weeks in the service," he said. He hesitated for a moment "In fact, considering the way she feels about her time at Fort Belvoir, which is where something pretty bad must have happened, I was surprised when she said she wanted to go with me to Brandywine. She normally won't even go shopping at Tyson's Corner."

He then went on to telling me about his wife's background. She was approaching thirty-one at the time they met to his sixty-four, but there'd been chemistry between them, and after six months of dating, he proposed, and she accepted. She'd transferred her Towson State credits to the University of the District of Columbia and had attended classes sporadically for six years. At the time of her disappearance, she was six credits short of her degree.

He gave me a photograph of her from his wallet. She looked younger than thirty-seven, much younger, with long brown hair that curled up at her shoulders, and framed an oval face with large, expressive eyes. She looked directly at the camera with an expression of supreme self-confidence. Except for the long hair and expensive clothing, she looked like a combat veteran. There's that look in the eyes that even the camera picks up on; the look that says 'I've been there and survived, and nothing can scare me now.'

"When was this picture taken?" I asked.

"Less than a year ago," he said. "We were at a resort in upstate New York, where I was interviewing the owner of a vineyard." He laughed. "I know what you're thinking. She looks so young in that photo. That's the way she looked when I met her, and that's the way she looked ten days ago, the last time I saw her, and you're wondering how a pale weakling like me became involved with a beauty like that."

That's precisely what I had been thinking, but having taken him on as a client, I didn't think it a good business idea to tell him that.

"No, not really," I said. "I just need to have a good idea what she looks like. Now, tell me about her habits, family, friends, things that will help me determine any patterns I might be able to look for."

"Her parents died when she was in high school," he said. "Her younger sister, Laura, is her only living relative."

"Were they in frequent contact?"

He shrugged. "Laura is two years younger than Leana. Their parents died the year Leana graduated high school, so she had to go to work to support Laura until she graduated. Laura's a bit of a . . . prima donna, but Leana has always felt responsible for her. She lived in Baltimore until last year, and then she moved here to DC. She works for an advertising agency. As for friends, Leana is a very private person. I honestly can't tell you if she's made any close friends since we married."

"I'll need Laura's full name and address."

"It's Laura Colman," he said. "Just like Leana she has no middle name. Their parents weren't exactly very imaginative." He gave me her address, a townhouse off Twenty-Fifth Street a few blocks west of the George Washington University Hospital.

"Did your wife have any favorite activities, or places she liked to hang out?"

He paused for a long interval before answering. "She liked to read, and she'd spend hours at art galleries or museums. She particularly fancied the Freer Gallery on the Mall." I wrote 'art galleries and museums' in my notebook.

So far, I didn't have a lot to go on. I would, of course, check with the sister, but I had to assume that the cops would have already done that.

"Now, I want you to go over with me the events on the day your wife went missing," I said. "Try not to leave anything out. Even the most insignificant detail can be important."

He began another recital of that day's events in a tired voice. When he got to the part about her wanting to tour the vineyard, I stopped him. "Were the two of you alone when this happened?" I asked.

He screwed up his eyes in concentration. "No, as a matter of fact, the door to our suite was ajar and the inn manager, Paul Cobane, was standing just outside."

I wrote Cobane's name in my notebook. "So, he overheard your . . . conversation?"

"He'd have to be deaf not to," he said. His cheeks reddened. "I'm afraid we were rather loud."

"Did you and your wife have rows like this often?"

"If you mean did we argue, of course we did. What married couple doesn't? In our case, we're both very passionate people, so when we do disagree, it can be quite intense. But, I can assure you, it never went beyond words. We never went to bed angry. No, I was just concerned that she'd get sunburned, and she resented me treating her like she couldn't take care of herself."

"I'm not judging. I just need to know what happened. What, by the way, *do* you think happened after your wife left the hotel room?"

"I spoke with the deputy about that," he said. "He said there were three possibilities; she walked out on me, she was kidnapped, or . . . something worse happened to her." The anguish in his voice was clear, and unless he was a damn good actor, he was hurting. "I don't believe the first. I loved her, and she loved me. It's been ten days and there've been no ransom demands. So, that leaves . . ."

His voice just trailed off. It was as if he felt that by not saying it, it would go away. But, it wouldn't go away. And, he'd been right. When someone is missing, it's usually either voluntary or they've been taken, or they've been killed and the body disposed of. There's nothing particularly pleasant about any of these scenarios, but with the first two, there's always the hope, no matter how faint, of a successful resolution, or at least, knowing the person's still alive. The last; well, people talk a lot about closure, but I'm at a bit of a loss as to how you close the book on something like that. Once, when I worked in the Pentagon, just before I left the army, I accompanied a brigadier general to Corpus Christi, Texas, where he spoke with a veterans' group. In the audience were several people who were related to soldiers classified as MIA, or missing in action, from World War 2, and the Korean and Vietnam Wars. The pain when they discussed their losses, and the difficulty of being unable to say a proper farewell, was just as deeply etched into the faces of the World War 2 families as those from recent wars. I could relate to that in a way. My parents were washed away in a hurricane that hit the Texas Gulf coast, and their bodies were never found. I'm not a religious person, but there is something missing when you don't have even a marble headstone to mark the passing of someone who was close to you.

So, I could understand the anguish Sonnenberg had to be feeling. If there'd been no ransom demand, and no kidnapper is likely to wait ten days; that left two options: she ran away, or someone did her in. I wouldn't rule out her deciding to cut and run from a man reaching the bottom of the downslope of his life, but, at the same time, I had to keep the third possibility in mind. Leana Sonnenberg's body could be decomposing in a shallow grave somewhere in the woods of northern Virginia; thousands of square miles and I didn't have a clue as to where to start looking. That also left the other depressing, but all too often correct, fact. When a person is killed, the chances of the murderer being a close relative, such as a spouse, are extremely high. I had to keep an open mind about it, though. For now he was a paying client. If he turned out to be something else, I'd cross that bridge when I came to it. Besides, he wasn't giving off the vibes of a man who'd killed his wife. That was

what I'd missed in the previous case. The ass
hole hadn't killed his wife, and I missed any
signals that he was planning to kill her until
it was almost too late.

"Let's stay positive about this," I said. "For
now, we'll just assume that your wife's out
there somewhere. Maybe she fell and hit her
head, and wandered off with amnesia.
Sounds strange, but it happens. Just to cover
all bases, though, can you think of anyone
who would want to do your wife harm?"

"No, I can't think of anyone who didn't
think the world of her," he said. "Of course, I
don't know what kind of relationships she
might have had with her classmates or
teachers at school. I've never met any of
them."

It wasn't totally lost on me that he'd used
the past tense when referring to her
relationships. I decided to test him.

"Why do you say the relationships she
had?" I asked.

He looked puzzled. "I don't understand."

"You referred to your wife's school
relationships in the past tense, as if they no
longer exist. Why is that?"

He pursed his lips and nearly closed his
eyes. "Why, you're correct," he said. "I guess .
. . oh, who am I kidding? I know Leana didn't
run off, and it doesn't look like she's been
kidnapped. You and I both know that leaves
only one other logical answer."

"You think your wife's dead?"

He was skinny, but when I said that, he seemed to deflate and become even smaller. His shoulders slumped and his eyes glistened. "What other answer is there?" There was anguish in his voice.

"But, if you think that, why are you hiring me to look for her?"

He rubbed at his temples. Suddenly, he looked like the tired, old man that he was.

"I guess I want you to find out what happened to her," he said. "If she's dead, I want you to find out who killed her."

I held my hand up to shut him off. "That's a job for the police, not a private investigator."

"Please, Mr. Pennyback," he said. "We both know that if they discover that Leana's been murdered, I will become their number one suspect. The fact is, the husband's quite often the guilty party, which guarantees that; and once they start looking at me, what do you want to bet that they won't look too hard in any other direction?"

He had a good point there. Cops are as human as the rest of us, and once they're convinced that they've found the right suspect, it's like pushing a rope up a hill to change their minds. Human nature can be a bitch. Once people make up their minds, they have a tendency to filter out anything that doesn't agree with what they've decided. When those people have the power to relieve you of your freedom, or even your life in extreme circumstances, it's truly frightening.

"Okay, I'll take the case, but you need to know this going in; if I find that your wife's been murdered, and that you're the guilty party, I'll turn you over to the cops in a heartbeat."

He looked me directly in the eye. His gaze and voice were steady when he said, "Quincy Chang said the same thing when he recommended you. When will you start working the case?"

I slammed my notebook shut. "What do you think we've been doing for the past hour?"

Charles Ray

FOUR

I assured Sonnenberg that Heather and I would do our best for him. I don't normally make snap decisions, and I have to confess that I wasn't too fond of him, but I was convinced that he'd been telling me the truth, as far as he knew it, and that if something bad had happened to his wife, he wasn't the one who'd done the deed. Now, all I had to do was deliver on my promise.

I had Heather call the number he'd given me for Laura Colman, and luckily she caught her at home. She made arrangements for me to go immediately and talk to her.

The weather was nice, and I wasn't sure about parking in Foggy Bottom. Parking in the area is limited to two hours unless you have a residential sticker in your window, and I couldn't be sure how long I'd take to talk to Colman, so I decided to walk up to the Waterfront Metro Station and take the subway.

Despite it being 10:30 in the morning, the city-bound platform for the Green Line was crowded with an assortment of business types in rumpled suits and laborers of both sexes with tired looks, dressed in scrubs, oil-stained overalls, and dusty jeans. After the train rolled in and discharged a handful of passengers, I found an empty seat at the end of the second car from the end for the four-minute ride to L'Enfant Plaza Station, where I got out and took the escalator up to the platform for the Blue and Orange Lines. There were even more waiting passengers for the trains heading in toward the center of the city, and I had to share a forward-facing seat with a heavyset woman wearing hot pink hospital scrubs. Most of the passengers got off at Metro Center, but my seatmate stayed in place until we arrived at the Foggy Bottom/GWU Station where we both got off. At the top of the escalator, she turned left into the George Washington University Hospital whose main entrance is only a few feet away, and I wormed my way through a couple of young women passing out PETA leaflets and an old guy selling limp looking bunches of roses and made my way through a crowd of students, hawkers and tourist gawkers to the walkway toward Twenty-Fifth Street. By the time I reached the sidewalk at Twenty-Fourth Street, the crowd had disappeared, and I didn't encounter a single pedestrian until I caught up with an old lady lugging two large shopping bags across New Hampshire Avenue. I considered offering to carry them for her, but the evil eye look she gave me as she turned and saw me closing in on her changed my mind. I merely smiled and walked quickly past her, crossed New Hampshire, and took a right when I got to Twenty-Fourth, looking back just as I turned to see her still staring at me.

Laura Colman lived in a narrow, two-story red brick townhouse that had steep, unevenly spaced brick steps up from the sidewalk. Two large urns containing sickly looking evergreens sat on the six-inch high concrete wall that around a concrete platform, about the size of a decent coat closet, which served as the house's front porch. The door, its red paint peeling, had three arched windows at eye level, and centered beneath them was a tarnished brass door knocker; a lion's head with a ring in its mouth. I saw no sign of a doorbell button, so I lifted the knocker and tapped it three times against the brass plate. It made a hollow sound. I tried peering through one of the windows, but the shimmery pattern of the glass, along with a layer of grime only revealed abstract patterns of dark and light. One of the dark patterns grew larger as it neared the door.

A few seconds later the door swung inward. I assumed I'd been eye-balled through the little hole in the door in the center of the brass ring and deemed no threat. Actually, Heather had probably described me when she called to make the appointment.

Standing in the half light from outside, framed by the door, Laura Colman looked so much like Leana Sonnenberg I just stood there for a few seconds with my mouth half open.

She had the same long brown hair, but it didn't curl quite as much, and the eyes were just as large, but had a world weary look. She wore a white dress shirt that was a size too large that draped over faded jeans that looked a size too small. Her half smile created dimples in both cheeks and tiny lines that radiated out from the corners of her eyes.

"You gonna stand there staring at me," she said. "Or will you introduce yourself and come in?"

The entranceway was a narrow space, wide enough for a stairwell to the second floor and a passage to the next room just wide enough for one person. A doorway to the left opened into a tiny sitting room dominated by a couch and a coffee table. She turned into the sitting room, and I followed. She indicated the end of the couch nearest the door and sat at the other end without waiting for me to sit.

As I squeezed in between the couch and coffee table, I took my ID out and held it out for her to see. "Thanks for agreeing to see me," I said.

She waved the ID away.

"I don't need to see that," she said. "Your secretary gave me a pretty good description of you when she called . . . and I must say, she really nailed it." She grinned at me.

"Ms. Bunche is my partner, not my secretary," I said. I decided to ignore the second part of her remark, which didn't soften my response. She frowned.

"Your partner; and *she* is the one who calls to make your appointments?" A bit of tension in her voice.

This was getting off to a bad start, and I had myself to blame. I should have just ignored her remark about Heather, but it always gets to me more than it does her when people just assume she's a secretary.

"She's a lot better with people on the phone than I am. We each do what we do best. I'm a disaster with paperwork, but do okay on the street or in face-to-face encounters. I guess you could say I'm the brawn and she's the brain of our company."

That last remark seemed to placate her. Her wolfish grin came back. "I can agree with that . . . the brawn part, I mean. So, what's the important matter that your partner couldn't tell me about on the phone?"

Heather hadn't told me that she'd not informed Colman of the real reason I wanted to talk to her. Just another example of her ability to get people to do things for her. I was going to have to let her work cases on the street more.

"I've been hired to look into your sister's case," I said.

The smile vanished from her face like someone had flipped a switch.

"You mean her murder, don't you? Why would a private investigator be involved . . . oh, that slime ball, Jackass hired you, didn't he?" "Jackass?"

"As in Jacob 'the Jackass' Sonnenberg."

"I take it you don't care much for your brother-in-law. Why did you say your sister was murdered? Right now she's only missing."

"She's been *missing* for nearly two weeks," she said. She made a sniffing noise. "I watch enough TV to know that's not a good sign. So, why'd he hire you?"

And here we'd been about to get along so well, and like a hairpin turn on a mountain road that catches you unawares, we were on opposite sides again. Heather would know how to smooth any ruffled feathers, but Heather wasn't here. I was flying solo through a dense fog.

"He hired me to find her . . . or find out what happened to her."

She made that sniffing sound again, only this time it was closer to a snort. "You mean he hired you to establish an alibi for him."

I deliberately raised my brows and leaned

in toward her.

"What makes you think he'd do a thing like that?" I let my voice rise at the beginning and trail off, hoping she'd take that for shock. I'd considered the same thing myself and discarded it. Sonnenberg came off as sincere, despite a bit of arrogant snarkiness, and I was convinced that he'd not harmed his wife. On the other hand, I was always prepared to admit when I'd figured things wrong, and here was someone much closer to those involved than me, and from whom I could possibly learn something. "He seemed to be genuinely concerned when he hired me."

Her expression softened. I kept mine neutral.

"There's nothing definite," she said. "Except the fact that Jacob's a control freak, and Leana was a free spirit who refused to be caged, so if anything bad has happened to her, he'd be the first person I'd look to." I noticed that she, too, pronounced her sister's name with three syllables.

I didn't have to fake my look of confusion. "Explain, please, how that translates to him hurting her, or worse, killing her."

"So, do you really think she's still alive? I haven't heard from her since the day before they went to that place down in Virginia, and that's not like her to stay out of touch for such a long time."

"Other than her husband, who I sense you suspect of doing something, do you know anyone who might want to do her harm?"

I'll give her credit. She really seemed to be thinking about it. "No, I don't know anyone who didn't like her. Leana was . . . is a wonderful person. Everyone who knows her loves her."

I decided to play devil's advocate to feel her out. "Wouldn't that include her husband?"

"I'm not saying that he didn't . . . doesn't . . . love her." Her face took on a wry expression. "In his own twisted way I think he loved her very much. Maybe a bit too much, if you know what I mean."

"Pretend that I don't," I said. "Please explain."

She stood suddenly. "Sure, but where are my manners? Would you like a cup of tea or coffee? I could use something refreshing right about now."

She was already moving crabwise to get from between the coffee table and sofa.

"I'll have whatever you're having, coffee or tea, it's fine with me," I said to her back as she went through a small arched doorway, turned right and moved out of sight.

In such a small house, I could hear the clang of metal in what I knew would be a tiny kitchen adjacent to the room she'd passed through, which would be a dining room large enough to hold a table and four to six chairs, and maybe a small side table for storing tableware. While waiting, I amused myself by studying the sitting *cum* living room. A small, rectangular space, the large sofa, coffee table, and a small case with double doors on the bottom half and two shelves on the upper half, made it look even smaller. The walls were covered by greenish-beige wallpaper with a dark green and off-white pattern of ivy vines and leaves, creating the impression of a small cave. There was also a smell in the air, a kind of mustiness, almost like the smell you encounter in the homes of the extremely old, but with a stinging undertone. The air was still, and I could see flickering dust motes hanging suspended in a shaft of light stabbing through the slit in the heavy curtains covering the window in the front wall. It was not a house I would have ordinarily associated with a woman in her early thirties.

After a few minutes, she came back carrying a brown plastic cafeteria tray upon which were two large white mugs, one with a triangular chip in the rim, several packets of sugar like those you find in fast food joints, and two mismatched stainless steel spoons. She put the tray on the coffee table, and handed me the cup without the chip.

"It's green tea," she said. "Better for you than coffee. Would you like sugar with yours?"

I sniffed the dark brown liquid. The aroma was mild, and not too bad; kind of like grass covered with early morning dew. I would have preferred coffee, but, when in Rome. "No, this is fine," I said. I took a sip. It *tasted* a bit like wet grass. I looked for a coaster, but noticed that the surface of the coffee table was covered in faint gray rings, so I put my cup down. "Now, we were talking about your sister's relationship with her husband."

She took several sips of tea before responding. "I . . . I guess it was okay when they first met," she said. "She loved him despite the age difference. I tried telling her it was a mistake, but Leana was . . . is, oh damn, I can't make up my mind whether to refer to her in the past tense or not; anyway, she was so stubborn, and so in love. She wouldn't listen." She twisted around on the sofa, and stared intently at me. "You know, Leana took care of me after our parents died. She put off going to college so she could work and support me until I graduated high school. Then, after I graduated and went to college, she joined the army to earn money to pay my tuition." Her eyes glistened and her lips quivered. "She's all I have left in this world."

A lot of people say that they know how you're feeling when they really have no clue. But, having lost my wife and six-year-old son in a senseless and totally avoidable traffic mishap, I knew exactly how she felt. She was hurt and angry, and she needed to hit out at someone. I wondered how much of her antipathy toward Sonnenberg stemmed from her honest belief that he was capable of harming his wife, and how much from that reflexive tendency to strike at the nearest target. After all, he'd incurred her ire in the first instance by taking her sister away from her. The detective in me, however, would follow every clue; even those that seemed to contradict my beliefs.

"You still haven't explained why you think he might have done something to her," I said gently.

"Like I said, he's a control freak. When Leana was in the army stationed at Fort Meade, and I lived in Baltimore, she used to stay at my apartment every weekend when she wasn't on duty. The year after she got transferred down to Fort Belvoir, I got this job here in DC as a freelance copy writer, and she used to come up and stay here. You know, she'd been talking about staying in the army for twenty years, but then eight years ago, she just up and quit. She went back to Baltimore and started going to Towson. She'd still come down here on weekends . . . I mean, I couldn't just quit my job and move back up there, now could I? She met Jackass, er, Jacob, at some kind of do they were having up there, and next thing I know, they're getting married, she drops out of Towson and moves down here. It was nice at first, having her close again, but he started objecting to her spending time with me. She almost had to sneak out to see me a few times a month."

"Why do you think he didn't want the two of you together?"

"Because he's a damn control freak," she said. "Didn't I already say that?"

"Okay, assuming that you're right; he's a control freak, and he didn't want his wife seeing her sister, and I admit, that seems kind of freaky; that doesn't mean he'd have any reason to hurt her."

She regarded me with a flinty glare over the rim of the mug. "Well, who else would have a reason to hurt her?"

"That, Ms. Colman, is what I intend to find out."

FIVE

I spent a total of three hours talking to Laura Colman, running well past my normal lunch time. So, needlessly to say, my stomach was growling by the time I got back to the Foggy Bottom Metro Station on Twenty-Third Street. Even though I knew Heather would give me grief for it, I stopped at one of the food trucks, fondly called Roach Coaches by the locals, that park on the sidewalk in the area, and bought a pork link sandwich, a big of barbecue flavor chips, and a Fanta grape drink, which I ate sitting the low stone wall in front of the huge gray building across the plaza from the hospital. A homeless guy, one of the hundreds inhabiting the city's streets since Reagan cut all federal funding for mental health care, dumping people out who were incapable of taking care themselves, sat down on the wall about four feet away from me, far enough away not to appear menacing, but not far enough to keep the rank odor of his unwashed body from reaching me. I offered to buy him a meal if he'd go elsewhere and eat it. He immediately took me up on my offer, and kept his word by moving south to the next block to eat it.

I smelled like a cheap roadside diner after a fire when I arrived back at the office, earning me a sniff and sneer from Heather, but thankfully she decided not to lecture me about my terrible eating habits.

Before grabbing my car keys from my desk and calling it a day, I sat down next to Heather's desk to map out our strategy for the case.

"First thing I want you to do," I said. "Is a full background check on Jacob Sonnenberg, Leana Colman Sonnenberg, and Laura Colman."

"You think either the husband or the sister might be involved?"

"No, actually, but it'll help me understand Leana better. Next up, I want to know as much about Brandywine Estates as possible."

She looked surprised—and confused.

"Look, she went missing there, missing without a trace. That alone is a good reason to check them out."

"Good point," she said. "Anything else?"

I was about to say no, then a thought hit

me. "Leana Sonnenberg was in the army, and was stationed not far from here. See what you can dig up about her time in the military."

She didn't ask me why this time, and I was thankful for that. I wouldn't have been able to explain it. Some people call it intuition, others call it gut instinct. Whatever you call it, something both her husband and her sister had said kept nagging at me. She was planning to do her twenty and retire, and then, halfway home she up and quits and didn't even explain why to her sister. Did it have anything to do with her being missing? Probably not, but it was a puzzle that needed solving. I hate unsolved puzzles. I know, I already said that, but it bears repeating.

Heather dismissed me in her usual manner. She simply turned her attention to her computer and acted as if I wasn't there. I took the hint, and left for home.

Driving crosstown from Southwest to Canal Road just below Georgetown University wasn't much trouble because at that time of day everyone in my area is going south or north to get out of the District. Once you hit M Street off Whitehurst Freeway, though, it's an inchworm parade of cars, vans, and pickups heading for the western and northwestern suburbs. It took me forty-five minutes to get from the start of Canal Road to the I-495/River Road turnoff, and twenty minutes from there through Potomac Village to the farmhouse off River Road that I call home.

There are few lights along my stretch of River Road, and none at all on the winding, gravel lane that leads off the road to my house, a one-story frame house that was built in the 1930s by an old farmer who, after he died, his surviving sons put up for sale. I got it for just below market value, along with the thirty acres of high grass and woodland that the old man had been unable to cultivate in his declining years, and a large barn with a galvanized tin roof and heavy wood sides. Both the house and barn were in good shape when I bought the place, and except for upgrades to the kitchen, the electrical system, and the addition of a security system for the windows and doors, I'd had little work to do to turn it into a nice, secluded place to get away from the clamor of the city. I'd lived alone for almost ten years before meeting Sandra Winter, a stunning, athletic blonde who worked as a teacher in one of the District's poorest high schools in one of its most depressed districts.

I met Sandra when I was hired by the grandmother of one of her students to investigate his murder. He'd been gunned down on the street not far from the house where he lived with her, and the police had written it off as just another gangbanger hit, common enough occurrences in many of the city's poorer neighborhoods, but the grandmother knew better, and was adamant that I prove the cops wrong. It turned out that she was right. The lad had just been in the wrong place at the wrong time—and, not the street where he was gunned down. He'd been one of Sandra's star pupils, with a load of artistic talent, and she allowed him to visit her home in Takoma Park, in the northwest part of the city, where he would sit in her back yard and draw sketches of her plants and flowers. One day, he'd accidentally witnessed her neighbor engaged in conversation with two thugs with whom he operated an art theft ring. Unfortunately, they'd spotted him, and the neighbor had the two track him down, and silence him permanently. In the course of my investigation, I'd foolishly intimated that Sandra had somehow been involved, which got our relationship off to a rocky start. I later discovered my mistake, almost too late, and in the course of being kidnapped along with me, Sandra had forgiven my mistake, and the rest, as they say, is history.

We've been more or less living together for several years now. She finally moved the last of her things from her Takoma Park house and rented it out, and moved in with me. So far, though, that's all the commitment either of us has made.

Ours is a somewhat complicated relationship. We like being together, but neither of us is quite ready to take that next step. Me because I've not completely gotten over the loss of my wife and son, and her because she's been accustomed to being on her own, and is not quite ready to surrender her independence. So, we just take it one day at a time. For all the apparent lack of commitment, we have a solid relationship, having tacitly decided to be exclusive. The physical side is great, but at our ages, not the defining aspect of our feelings for each other. More than lovers, we're friends; sharing ourselves on a deeper level than can be attained by sex alone. I find myself looking forward to coming home to her, and I think she feels the same way.

That feeling was intensified when I turned the last curve in the gravel lane and the lights of the house came into view. A warm, yellow glow seemed to envelope it, making it stand out from the towering darkness of the trees like a campfire after a long hike, and it caused me to press a little harder on the gas pedal to hurry my arrival.

I pulled into my usual spot next to the front porch. Sandra's car, a light blue Honda Civic that she bought recently, was already there. The light from the living room was visible through a slight gap in the heavy curtains that Sandra insisted on keeping closed at night, despite the fact that we were so far from the main road only a trespasser would even be able to see the house, much see inside. I opened the front door and stepped inside. The outside temperature in May in the DC area is usually cool because of the amount of moisture in the air, so the warmth of the living room was welcome.

The living room was well-lit, but empty. I heard sounds from the kitchen, so I went that way. Sandra, dressed in short shorts that accented the roundness of her buttocks and a tee shirt that barely contained her breasts, unconstrained by a bra, was cleaning out the refrigerator. She stood with her feet spread apart amid the contents which were arrayed around her on the floor. I just stood there in the door for a few seconds, watching her stretch to reach the back of the fridge above the top shelf, admiring how the muscles and curves of her body moved against the thin fabric.

"Hey, lady," I said quietly. "You're gonna have to take a long hot shower if you're going out to eat Thai with me tonight."

She pulled back from her work and turned to face me, and swiped at a stray lock of blonde hair that had escaped the loose pile she tied up on top of her head.

"Seriously? You couldn't call me at school and warn me?" Her broad smile, though, took all of the sting out of her rebuke.

"I wanted to surprise you, babe. How'd I know you were gonna go all spring cleaning on me?"

"Fair enough," she said. "Help me put this stuff back, and then you can help me scrub my back." The smile now wasn't as broad, but much more meaningful, and the look in her eyes told me she wanted more than a back scrub.

Putting everything back was a task that was done quickly and without regard to neatness, and we raced each other to the bathroom. An hour later, we were dressed and in my car.

Canal Road, which is one-way inbound in the morning, and one-way outbound during the evening rush, becomes two-way again after 6:00, so we were able to dodge the Beltway traffic and get into Rosslyn across the Key Bridge. That part of Northern Virginia pretty much shuts down at night, not picking up again until you've driven west on Wilson Boulevard for four or five blocks. The older part of Arlington is home to a lot of smaller, independently owned restaurants, jewelry shops, bars, and fast food joints that cater to the working class stiffs who live in the red brick townhouses squatting on the residential streets north and south of the main thoroughfare. Taste of Thai is a small Thai restaurant jammed into a dingy strip mall along with a shoe repair shop, a Vietnamese restaurant and an adult book store. The parking lot slopes downward toward the street and when the eateries are crowded—most nights—it's tricky to turn into one of the slanted parking spaces without scraping your car's finish on one of your neighbors. That's why I like my Volkswagen. It turns on a dime and fits into a shoebox.

"*Sawasdee-ka,*" the diminutive Thai waitress said as we entered. She held her hands together just below her nose in the traditional Thai *wai,* or greeting of respect. "Welcome to Taste of Thai. You would like a table for two?" Her switch from Thai to English was seamless, and her accent was hardly noticeable.

We nodded and followed her to a table off to the right in the corner. It was set up for four, but she quickly removed the extra implements and asked if we wanted drinks while we looked at the menu.

"*Song bia Singh,*" I said, ordering two bottles of the imported Thai beer, Singha.

The waitress beamed at me. "*Khun phut pasa Thai di mak,*" she said, although I knew that I didn't actually speak the language all that well. The tones gave me trouble. But, in Asian culture, one must humbly acknowledge compliments.

"Oh, no," I said. "My Thai is *mai di.* I only know a few words."

"Where did you learn to speak Thai?"

"When I was in the army, many years ago, I used to work with the Thai army," I said. "I took a few lessons, and picked up a lot from the guys I worked with."

She made a few more encouraging comments about my linguistic ability before scurrying off to get our beers. Sandra smiled indulgently at me. She was accustomed to my habit of using a few words of the various languages that I know a few words of to ingratiate myself with the servers at ethnic restaurants. It was the respectful thing to do, and when you consider that the average American thinks the rest of the world should learn to speak English and that the way to make a foreigner understand you is speak slower and louder, it's a no-fuss way to distinguish yourself. Besides, it usually got us first class service.

We'd discussed what we wanted to eat during the drive, so when the waitress brought our drinks, we ordered. For appetizers, we got chicken *satay,* which consists of strips of fried white chicken meat on wooden skewers served with a sweet brown peanut sauce. Our main course was *som tam,* a salad made of slices of green papaya with noodles, onions and other greens; pork *pad tay* with pieces of grilled meat and assorted spicy vegetables; *tom yang gung,* a soup with shrimp, lemon grass and other spices; beef *pad prew wan,* which is chunks of beef with peppers, onions and assorted herbs; and white rice. The appetizers came quickly, and we pitched right in. The rest of the food was just as quick, which, along with the taste, is why we like Thai food. We were just finishing the last *satay* when the waitress arrived with a tray laden with our order along with a little caddy of Thai condiments, including those tiny green peppers, *prik khi nu,* which they translate as rat shit pepper, and a couple of other small bottles of stuff I didn't recognize.

I have no favorite Asian cuisine, but Thai food would be near the top of any list I was forced to make. It tastes good, and I love the Thai eating style. You can ask for chopsticks; the Chinese introduced the instrument to Thailand over a thousand years ago, but the traditional way to eat Thai food is to use a fork to shove the food onto a spoon from which you eat. A practical way to eat that the average *farang,* or foreigner, can master, unlike chopsticks that require a certain manual dexterity that many westerners find challenging. Sandra and I are the exception to that. When we eat at Korean or Chinese restaurants, we always insist on chopsticks. I'd learned to use them during my deployments to Asia, and she'd learned after watching me once or twice.

We'd been busy with the appetizers, so we didn't get around to the ritual of sharing our respective days until we'd scooped generous amounts of all the dishes onto our plates and taken our first bites.

"So, how were things at school today?" I asked after taking a sip of beer to wash down the spoonful of *pad prew wan.*

For the next few minutes, Sandra regaled me with tales of high school students a few weeks away from summer vacation, and how hard it is to get, much less hold, their attention under those circumstances. The only good thing, she said happily, is that they're so excited about the end of school they don't get into as many fights.

"Now," she said when she'd finished. "What mischief did you get up to today?"

"I'm not sure you could call it mischief, but it's certainly strange." I then outlined the day's events for her, including my meeting with Laura Colman.

"Laura Colman sounds like a troubled woman," she said when I'd finished. Just like a veteran teacher to cut right to the chase.

"I sort of got the same feeling. I just can't figure out what it is that's bugging me, though."

"Do you think Leana Sonnenberg's still alive?" Again, she gets right to what matters.

I could only shrug. This is the part of what I do and how I do it that confuses the hell out of most people—sometimes it even confuses me. "Statistically, after being missing for so long with no contact, she's either run away and doesn't want to be found, or she's dead. But, I've got this feeling deep in my gut that tells me she's still alive. I can't explain why, it's just a feeling."

"I'll take you and your gut feelings over most other people's intellect any day." She laughed. "I've seen you right too many times to doubt. You did, however, miss at least one other possibility."

"What? She's either runaway or she's dead; what else could there be?"

She gave me a look that I figure she must have perfected on hardheaded high school students. "She's missing, babe. That's a general condition, not a cause. *Why* is she missing? Did she run away? You don't seem to think so. Was she kidnapped? There's been no ransom demand, so that would seem to be out. Was she killed? Possibly, but your gut tells you no. There is, however, one other possibility."

"And, that is?"

"That someone wants her to be missing. Not dead, just out of circulation."

Damn! That's just one of the reasons I love this woman. Beauty and brains, and a small bit of feminine brawn; she's the total package.

Charles Ray

SIX

The next morning, I was up at 5:30 as usual. I roused Sandra from a sound sleep, and we changed into our running gear. We did our four-mile-run through the woods, not talking, but focused on our own thoughts. The run was effortless for the most part, only taxing us at the end, just over a mile of a gently upslope, which is easy to walk, but can be a bit of a strain on calf muscles already tired from three miles of running at a steady but demanded pace. Our legs were tight, but not sore, when we pulled up in front of the barn, so we jogged in place for five minutes to let muscles and breathing settle. This was followed by a thirty-minute workout on the heavy bag in the gym. We worked the bag routine together, taking turns kicking and punching from opposite sides until our calves were thrumming again.

I sat on the back porch and meditated while she showered, and I showered while she cooked breakfast. We ate in silence. She knew I was thinking about the case, so she said nothing, just occasionally running her hand lightly across my shoulder as she passed me, or laying it gently on my arm as I sat there staring off in the middle distance, eating my bacon, scrambled eggs and toast on auto-pilot.

It was only as I was draining the last of my coffee that I was ready to rejoin the world we shared.

"I going to Brandywine Estates and have a look around," I said.

"That seems like a good idea," she said. "Get a look at the scene of the crime, so to speak. What do you think you'll find after more than ten days, though?"

Good question. Probably nothing. But, you never know.

"I have no idea. I won't know until I get there." After so long there wouldn't be any physical evidence left anyway.

She looked at me, her coffee cup halfway from the table to her mouth. "Another one of your gut feelings?"

"Not really," I said. "I just want . . . no, need to get a sense of the layout of the place. It's an inn and they had some kind of event planned, which means there had to be other guests. How does a person go missing in a situation like that and no one notices? I need to see the place myself to figure out how that could have happened."

She made a 'hm' sound and sipped her

coffee. I shrugged and started clearing the dishes from the table. After a few seconds, she joined me at the sink and helped me finish cleaning things up.

We left together at 7:40, with her following me until we approached the Bureau of Engraving and Printing on Independence Avenue. She kept to the left to get to Carver High School, and I went right to make my way to Maine Avenue and my office.

After checking in with Heather, and learning that she'd turned up nothing interesting, I hopped back in the Volkswagen for the drive to Brandywine Estates. I asked Heather to call them to let someone know I was coming and why. Under the circumstances, it didn't make any sense to try and conceal anything from the people who were at the center of events, and if they knew in advance what I was up to, I could maybe get some sense of who knew what, or who might be concealing information. Long shot? Yeah, but when you have nothing to go on, a long shot is sometimes the only shot you have.

I drove to I-395 and south to the Beltway, and then west to US 29 south, through Fairfax and into the countryside. The chaotic sprawl of Northern Virginia's near suburbs, caused by uncontrolled development jamming housing estates, condos, office buildings and shopping malls together without regard to the ability of the transportation network to cope, lasts until a bit past Fairfax City. It then turns into semi-rural, with an odd mixture of wealth-induced gentility existing side by side with poverty-fueled decay. Over-priced housing communities, old mansions, rundown frame houses, machine shops, and rusted hulks of pickups mingle in relatively peaceful coexistence. Some parts are totally rural and bucolic, like the stretch of road through Manassas Battlefield Park, a sprawling national park that straddles the highway. I seldom visit this part of the state, but always enjoy the drive when I do. Unlike the western route, there are fewer gun shops or rickety roadside bars displaying Confederate flags, and with the horse farms and quaint looking small towns with their old buildings and narrow streets, it brings to mind what the area must have looked like during the last century. The people, too, seem to be a bit friendlier to strangers than their neighbors to the west.

I always pull into the little blacktop parking area just before the Stone House at the intersection of Route 29 and Sudley Road. This two-story, brick building was built in 1848 to serve as a stop on the Fauquier to Alexandria Turnpike. During the opening battles of the Civil War, the first and second battles of Manassas, also known as the Battles of Bull Run for the stream that flows through the area, it served as a hospital. I got out and leaned against the front of my car, scanning the rolling hills around me, imagining what it must have looked like on July 21, 1861, when Brigadier General Irvin McDowell marched 35,000 green Union recruits south from Washington with the intent of flanking the Confederate army and marching on Richmond. Just three months after the rebels had fired on Fort Sumter, starting the most deadly war the country has ever engaged in. Despite the fact that his troops were 90-day volunteers with little training, McDowell was confident of victory. So to was the citizenry of the nation's capital, many of whom packed picnic baskets and followed the army in their carriages to watch the 'show' as the Union army taught the rebels a lesson. The Confederates, however, in the early days of hostilities, proved to be a harder nut to crack than anyone anticipated. When the Union forces reached Bull Run, they came face to face with 22,000 rebels under the command of General Pierre G. T. Beauregard. General Joseph Johnston and his 10,000 rebel troops stationed in the Shenandoah Valley were ordered to redeploy and aid Beauregard. Although the Union forces had the upper hand at the outset, rebel stubbornness and experience in the field won out in the end and McDowell was forced to order a withdrawal. Orderly at first, when his troops encountered the panicked sightseers on the roads, they too lost control and the orderly withdrawal became a rout. It was a decisive victory for the Confederacy, but one the rebel commanders failed to take advantage of, so the war dragged on for four more years, leading to the bloodiest battles in our history, and a legacy of divisiveness that persists to this day. Manassas, or Bull Run, wasn't the Civil War's bloodiest battle, nor was it particularly decisive. But, for me, it vividly illustrates the folly of war. As I stood there, I could hear the screams of the wounded and dying, the crack of muskets and the boom of cannons; I could smell the stinging odor of gunpowder, the metallic tang of blood, the rank odor of sweat from fear, and the musk of voided bowels and bladders as men died. I'd never been in a battle that came close to anything that the veterans of that war had witnessed, not even a minor debacle like Bull Run, but I'd seen, heard, and smelled enough to be moved by it, and I wondered how many civilians, standing where I stood, thought the same thoughts. Probably none. Only soldiers, or people who have been caught up in a battle, can know what it's like.

Shaking myself to clear my thoughts, I got back in my car and continued my journey.

The turnoff to Brandywine Estates was on the left, five miles beyond the road leading to Vint Hill Farm Station, the old Army Security Agency base that was closed at the end of the Cold War in the early 1990s. The two-lane road wound lazily past stately horse farms and old antebellum mansions. Just before a large white wooden gate frame with a sign that arched over the roadway with the words 'Brandywine Estates' in Old English script written on it there was a large public park on the left side of the road with a few picnic tables and four brick barbecue pits, probably as close as any locals could ever get to the luxury that lay beyond the white fence. The gate was flung open and the place wasn't guarded, but then, I suppose vineyards aren't exactly prime targets for any kind of criminal activity unless it's someone who wants to steal grapes, and transporting the loot would present a logistical problem.

Long rows of grape vines held up by a series of poles and wires stretched away from the road on both sides for as far as the eye could see. There was a wide lane between each row of vines, confirming what I'd thought. Anyone in the vineyard only had to follow the path and it would eventually lead either to the white wood fence that seemed to enclose the place, or back to the road.

The road made a sharp turn to the right and Brandywine Inn stood before me. From a hundred yards away it looked like an oversized version of an antebellum mansion, with covered porches around the first and second floor and a large *porte cochere* at the main entrance. As I got closer, I could see that it was indeed huge, a hundred yards across the front at a minimum. The large double doors of the main entrance were wide enough to drive a school bus through. A large parking lot off to the right held about ten expensive cars, and off to the left were several low outbuildings of various sizes, gleaming white like the main building with roofs covered in the same dark green tile. The parking lot near the outbuildings contained older cars and pickups, marking it as for employee parking. Sure enough, as I entered the circular drive the looped through the *porte cochere*, I saw a sign in the grass that read, 'Guest Parking' with an arrow pointing right, and 'Employee Parking' with an arrow pointing left.

My green Volkswagen would have been more at home in the employee lot, but being the contrarian that I am, I turned right and parked in the first empty space in the lot with the expensive cars. Hell, I was a visitor, not an employee. If anyone objected, they'd have to deal with it. No one came running out to tell me to move, so I cut the engine, got out and locked the car.

The walkway from the parking lot to the entrance steps was a wide red cobblestone affair bordered in red gardenias. I mounted marble steps up to the wraparound porch, or verandah, which had a floor of dark brown polished wood and marble railings. Black wrought iron tables and chairs with beige marble tops and seats were placed at intervals to the left and right on the verandah, and next to each table was a large blue and white Chinese vase containing red-blooming azalea plants surrounded at the base by lilac-colored hydrangeas. The entrance doors were dark wood with lead glass panes inset allowing a distorted view of the interior. They swung inward easily.

The lobby of the Brandywine Inn was as opulent as the entrance suggested.

A vaulted ceiling with a painting of an idyllic landscape loomed overhead. The floors were marble with expensive-looking Oriental carpets strewn haphazardly around. The dark wood walls were dotted with large framed oil paintings with stuffy looking gentlemen wearing a lot of lace collars and pinched waist jackets. To the front and right were chairs and chaise lounges done in brown and purple velvet, arranged around black wrought iron tables with black marble tops. The check-in desk, a waist-high platform of dark wood with marble top, ran almost the length of the room on the left. Two young women, one with shoulder-length over-large blonde hair, thick black brows, bright blue eyes and a sprayed-on tan, the other, her brown hair trimmed in a page boy cut framing an elfin face with a nose that was a bit too long and narrow, and no tan, both wearing white puffed collared blouses under black vests, stood behind the desk smiling out at the empty room. They looked like

Barbie dolls on display.

Their heads swung and they zeroed in on me as my shoes made clicking sounds on the marble floor. Rehearsed smiles creased their faces.

"Good morning, sir," the two Barbies said in unison. "Welcome to Brandywine Inn. How may we be of service?"

I pulled out my ID and held it up so they both could see it. "I'd like to talk to the manager," I said.

Two pairs of eyes went round, and their heads swiveled so that they were looking at each other. Their pink lips were rounded in little 'oohs'.

"Is there something wrong?" the Barbie on the right asked.

"I'd really rather discuss that with your manager," I said. "Can you direct me to him?"

The Barbie on the left picked up a phone. "I'll call him and let him know you'd like to talk to him," she said. She punched in a series of numbers and put her hand over the mouthpiece to murmur into the phone. After nodding her head, she put the phone down and smiled at me. "Mr. Cobane will be right out. If you'd like to have a seat." She pointed at the nearest table and chairs.

"Would you like a glass of punch?" her twin asked.

I waved her off and sat down. My butt hadn't had time to warm the chair's seat before a slender man wearing a dark gray suit with the silk triangle of a handkerchief peeking out of the breast pocket came striding across the lobby. He had a look about him that I recognized, a look I'd seen on hotel managers in every country I'd ever been; a man accustomed to meeting and greeting all kinds of people, and who, regardless of how he might be feeling, saw it as his duty to make you feel welcome.

"I'm Paul Cobane, general manager of Brandywine Inn," he said, his practiced smile in place "You wish to speak with me?" He extended a slender, well-manicured hand.

I stood and took his hand. "Yes, Mr. Cobane. Is there somewhere we can talk privately?"

He pulled his hand back rather quickly and looked at me with narrowed, suspicious eyes. For a moment, the façade of welcoming hotel manager disappeared, to be replaced by businessman who sees trouble coming. "Is this about the lady who turned up missing from here a couple of weeks ago?"

"Eleven days, but yes it does."

His face went pale. "Then, the person you really need to talk to is Harlan Cuthbert, the owner," he said. "If you'll follow me to my office, I'll call and let him know you're here."

SEVEN

Paul Cobane led me through the lobby, through the large formal dining room just beyond the curved stairwell leading to the mezzanine level, and down a long, carpeted hallway with doors on both sides, to a large door at the end with 'Paul Cobane, General Manager' in gold leaf on a pebbly black plaque.

The floor was covered in a thick green carpet with gold accents in the shape of ivy leaves. A large mahogany desk sat opposite the door. His chair was a much newer and more expensive version of the old second-hand chair I have in my office. The wall behind the chair was covered with certificates and photos of Cobane with various celebrities, and many looked like they'd been taken in exotic foreign locales. To the left was a glass and chrome bar with dozens of bottles of expensive liquor on a wall-mounted glass rack. The right-hand side of the office had a low, kidney shaped glass coffee table and three futuristic looking chairs. He motioned me to one of the chairs and went behind his desk. Like the girl at reception, he covered his mouth while he talked. After a brief conversation, he sat in the chair to my right.

"Harlan's down at the warehouse," he said. "He'll be here shortly. Would you like a drink while we wait?"

"I'll have a mineral water if you have it," I said. No way was I gonna let booze scramble my brains before talking to this guy and his boss.

"Sure, any particular brand?"

"Whatever you have."

He retrieved a bottle of Evian from a small refrigerator under the bar and poured it into a cut crystal glass over two cubes of ice. He put it on the table on top of a crystal coaster. He then went back to the bar and put ice and four fingers of Chivas Regal into another glass. He stirred the liquor with his finger and then licked it. He sat in the chair opposite me and took a long drink.

"So," I said after taking a sip of water. "While we're waiting for your boss, what can you tell me about the day Leana Sonnenberg disappeared?"

He held his glass in two hands. I could see little ripples in the surface of the golden liquor. His hands were shaking.

"Not a lot," he said finally. "I welcomed the

Sonnenbergs to the inn, of course. That's my duty as general manager. Because Mr. Sonnenberg is so important to the success of Harlan, er, Mr. Cuthbert's, new venture, I went the extra mile, and even escorted them to their suite. I passed along the invitation for them to join a few of the other guests for a tour of the vineyard guided by Mr. Cuthbert himself." He took another drink, a bit more restrained this time. "Mr. Sonnenberg declined the invitation, but, his wife jumped at the idea. That caused a little friction between them, but finally, Mr. Sonnenberg told her to go ahead and, let's see if I remember his words exactly . . . 'ruin your skin under a hot Virginia sun while someone else ruins your day prattling on about something they barely understand'. Anyway, she went off to join the tour and he stayed in his room. The next thing I know, he's coming to me complaining that she's missing."

He actually seemed to know quite a lot. Whether he didn't realize it, or was bullshitting me, remained to be seen.

"So, the Sonnenbergs argued? Did it get physical?"

"No, nothing like that," he said. "I'm not sure you could even call it an argument, really. He just suggested she'd be better off staying in the room, and she said she didn't come out to stay cooped up in the room, and he came back with the bit about the sun, and she flounced off. Believe me; I've seen couples go at it a lot worse than that. I guess that kind of disagreement is to be expected with a couple like the Sonnenbergs."

"What do you mean, a couple like the Sonnenbergs?" I asked.

"Come on, you've met him, right? A man as old as him married to a beautiful young woman like her . . . there's bound to be some insecurity on his part when she wants to go off alone with other people."

"Even jealousy?" I asked.

"Well, yeah. I know I'd be jealous if I was his age and my wife was a looker like Mrs. Sonnenberg. Anyway, why are you asking about that?"

"Just curious. So, she went off to join the tour. Where was it supposed to meet?"

"The equipment shed I think they call it, I know nothing about motors or machines," he said. "If you looked to your left as you drove in, you saw it; the medium-sized building adjacent to the employee parking lot. The group was to meet there and tour the north vineyards, which are the ones on the left side of the road you drove in on."

"Who was guiding the tour?"

"Harlan led the tour himself."

"Is that usual?"

"What's usual?" He shrugged. "Harlan's just getting his first batch of wine ready for market. Hell, the inn's only been open eighteen months, so the whole setup is really in a startup phase. That would have been . . .

was the first tour we'd ever done. In addition to Sonnenberg, we had a freelance writer working for the *New Yorker,* and a journalist for some other lifestyle publication. He wanted to impress them in the hopes they'd write glowing reviews of the place. The market's pretty much flooded with wines, and a new label needs all the hype it can get."

"Your boss must have been disappointed that Sonnenberg refused to go on the tour," I said.

"That's putting it mildly. He was royally pissed. Of course, he'd never say anything to Mr. Sonnenberg—he's not about to blow a chance of a good review of the wine, or the inn, and, of course, when Mrs. Sonnenberg turned up missing, any mention of his absence on the tour would have been quite inappropriate."

I wanted to make notes, but so far Cobane was at ease with me, and I didn't want to turn him off. I'd just have to remember things and try to write it down later.

"I understand Sonnenberg came to you first to report his wife missing?"

"Yeah, everyone comes to the general manager for everything." He laughed. "Oh, sorry, I guess that's not funny considering the circumstances."

"Hey, sometimes you just have to laugh," I said. "I know what you mean, though. You're the most responsible person around, so anything that happens is your responsibility."

He laughed louder. "Boy, did you nail it. Anyway, he came to me. The first thing I did was have the staff search the grounds, including the vineyards. When she didn't turn up, I personally called the Fauquier County Sheriff. Harlan chewed my ass royally for that, by the way."

"Someone goes missing, and he didn't want you calling the authorities?"

"I know it sounds bad, but put yourself in his place," he said. "He's sunk a lot of money into this place, and he was worried about the effect of negative publicity. To his credit, when the cops arrived, he cooperated fully. Let them search the place from top to bottom, including the wine storage area, and he usually doesn't let anyone in there."

"So, your people searched, the police searched, and nothing turned up?"

He shook his head. "Not a thing. It's like she just vanished into thin air."

His door opened and banged against the soft tip of the door stop with a dull thud. Cobane looked up and paled.

"So, Paul, what the fuck's so important you pull me away from my work?"

I turned. The voice was harsh, and strident, with tones of the upper northeastern United States. The florid face, small, close-set eyes, and wispy side hair combed over the top to hide a bald spot fit the voice. He was wearing a pair of faded jeans and a plaid shirt. He had the look of someone who had once worked out, but hadn't done so in a while. A pronounced pot belly pushed at the front of the shirt. I didn't need an introduction to know that this was Harlan Cuthbert.

Charles Ray

EIGHT

"Uh, Harlan," Cobane said. "This is Al Pennyback. He's a private investigator looking into Mrs. Sonnenberg's disappearance."

Cuthbert looked at me the same way you'd look at a piece of dog shit stuck to the bottom of your shoe. He didn't otherwise acknowledge my presence, or offer to shake hands, so I didn't bother standing.

"Why would a private eye be getting involved in a case like this?" I figured that question was addressed to me, even though he continued to glare at Cobane.

Cobane's gaze shifted from Cuthbert to me, his brow furrowed in confusion.

"It's been more than ten days since Leana Sonnenberg went missing," I said. "And, the police have found nothing. Needless to say, her husband is worried out of his mind. He's hired me to see if I can find something the police might have missed."

Cuthbert finally deigned to noticed me. His expression was anything but friendly. "You think you can do better than the police?" His voice dripped with sarcastic arrogance.

"I've been known to do that."

I don't like bragging, but that just happens to be the truth. Unlike the police, I don't have to worry about Miranda rights or search warrants . . . or probable cause, not that he really needed to know any of that.

"So, what do you want here?"

He was a hard man to impress. I guess they don't read the *Washington Post*. That's where my friend Lucy Garcia does the occasional article about my exploits. Lucy writes features for the *Post's* style and metro sections, and she'd been the reporter bird-dogging me after I worked the case of Sandra's student. She'd stressed in her article how I'd believed in an old woman when the system had failed her and her grandson, and dubbed me the 'Brown Knight.' Looking at the vein throbbing in Cuthbert's neck, I didn't think he'd be impressed, so I decided to stick to the standard pitch.

"Sometimes a fresh set of eyes will notice what the police might have missed," I said. "It's impossible for someone to occupy a space and not leave at least a trace of evidence. If you don't mind, I'd like to retrace

Ms. Sonnenberg's steps from her room to . . . wherever she might have gone."

He didn't look convinced.

"I'm sure your cooperation in this will influence Mr. Sonnenberg's article about your establishment, an article he hasn't yet written," I said. I didn't know if that was true, it probably wasn't true in fact, but if I read Cuthbert right, that was more important to him than the fate of Leana Sonnenberg. It worked. His expression loosened.

"Okay," he said. "Paul, you show him the room and the way to the shed. I'll meet you there and show you around the rest of the place."

He turned and left without waiting for either of us to acknowledge his instructions; a man accustomed to giving orders and having them carried out.

"Okay, if you'll follow me, I'll show you the room," Cobane said with the tone of someone who was chafing at having to obey orders like a low-level employee rather than the general manager he was.

We went back out to the lobby and up the staircase to the mezzanine, which held a cozy cocktail lounge with private booths and widely scattered tables with plushy chairs enabling the occasional *tete-a-tete* outside guest rooms. Beyond the lounge was a wide hallway that stretched to the far wall. The brass plaque over the entrance to the hallway identified this area as 'The Presidential

Promenade.' Cobane said that the hallway on the other side of the lounge was 'The Royal Boulevard.'

The Sonnenbergs had been assigned one of the best suites in the wing, at the end of the hallway. Cobane used a pass key to unlock the door, swung it open and stepped back for me to enter.

Oh, how the rich and famous live and travel.

The sitting room of the suite would hold my living room and kitchen. The pictures on the walls were originals, and the furniture was the kind of stuff you see in the ritzy lifestyle magazines, all fluff and lace and not actually made to be used. Beyond the sitting were a large bedroom with a four-poster bed big enough for a whole basketball to sleep in and an enormous bathroom with a step-in tub with whirlpool bath. It was all very interesting, but it didn't tell me where Leana Sonnenberg had gotten to.

"So," I said. "Where did she go from here?"

"That would be the equipment shed I told you about before. I'll show you the way."

We retraced our steps to the lobby and out through the main entrance. He turned right on the verandah. There were steps down at the end that I'd not noticed when I arrived. He led me across the employee parking lot to a medium sized metal building on the lot's periphery.

"The group was to meet Harlan right

about here, I believe," he said. "I have no idea where she went afterwards, other than hearing that she changed her mind about taking the tour and decided to visit our gardens instead."

"Where are the gardens located?"

He pointed toward the back side of the inn. "They're directly behind the main building. You can't miss them."

Before I could thank him, he walked away; quickly as if this was a part of Brandywine Estates that he wanted nothing to do with. The roll-up door of the building was rolled all the way up, and I could see inside. I recognized a tractor and a small wagon, but the other items were unrecognizable. In the back, I saw three shadowy figures in the gloom of the structure. They moved between the tractor and the wagon and emerged into the light.

Cuthbert was talking to the two men who flanked him; a tall, broad shouldered guy with medium brown skin and a military-style haircut, on his left, and a shorter, but just as broad-shouldered guy with short, blond hair on his right. He was frowning, and frowned deeper when he saw me, while they listened respectfully. When they were about ten feet away, Cuthbert stopped talking, but he continued to regard me with a frown on his face. The trio stopped four feet away; a neutral distance; close enough that if they spoke in a normal tone I could hear, but if they whispered, I'd be cut out of the conversation. Cuthbert's two companions eyed me coldly, not exactly hostile, but still challenging. I recognized them as former military from the haircuts.

"I hope I'm not interfering with anything important," I said to break the ice.

"Not a problem," Cuthbert said. "I reckon Jacob's pretty wrecked, with his wife missing and all. Anything we can do to help, you just name it." The words were right, but I didn't detect even a tiny bit of sincerity in his voice. "So, where do you want to start?"

"I guess with the tour she was supposed to join," I said. "Your manager said she came out here." I looked at Cuthbert. "You were leading that tour, right?"

"Yeah, it was supposed to be a way to break the ice with the journalists who were here covering the place." He frowned again. "Sonnenberg declined. I guess he thought he was too good for such a small time operation."

"But, Mrs. Sonnenberg agreed to go. What time did she show up?"

He looked at the blond. "I can't really tell you," he said. "This is Rob Lindsey, my vineyard manager. He was assembling the tour group. I had some business with Ken here." He nodded toward the other man. "Ken Bell's my chief mechanic. We were having some problems with the tractor motor, and I was discussing it with him, so I had Rob babysit with the tour until we were done. Rob, what time did Mrs. Sonnenberg show up?"

The blond ran a hand through his hair. "Uh, I think it was about four or five minutes before you joined us, Mister C," he said. "She showed up, looked around and then said she'd changed her mind, and she took off." He was talking to Cuthbert, but watching me out of the corner of his eye as he spoke.

"Did she say where she was going?" I asked him.

"Yeah, she said something about going to see the gardens," he said. "And, that's the way she went." He still refused to make direct eye contact with me.

"And, none of you saw her again after that?"

"That's right," Cuthbert said. "We did the tour, and forgot all about it until Sonnenberg told Paul she was missing."

"I understand that you immediately searched the place?"

"Rob and Ken led the search, yes," he said.

I looked at them.

"Rob took some workers and checked the vineyards, and me and one of my mechanics searched the buildings and grounds around the inn," Bell said. "We didn't see any sign of her."

"Same thing in the vineyard," Lindsey said.

"And then, of course, Paul called the sheriff and they came out and searched the place all over again, and just like us, found nothing," Cuthbert added.

"I hate to do this," I said. "But, would you mind walking me through your search?"

They frowned and looked at Cuthbert.

"What the hell for?" he asked. "You really think you might find something we missed?"

"It's impossible to say until I've walked the same ground you walked," I said. "But, sometimes a fresh pair of eyes can notice things that might have been seen but not thought pertinent at the time. Don't forget, you all, the police included, would have been tense and worried given the circumstances."

They shared looks, Cuthbert's two minions looking put upon, him just looking frustrated. His brow furrowed, and for a heartbeat I thought he'd refuse, but finally, he shrugged. "Fine, I guess it couldn't hurt to take another look. Where do you want to start first?"

Given what I'd been told, I didn't think Leana would have gone into the vineyard. "This area, the buildings—I assume you searched them as well—and the area around the garden."

"Yeah, we did. Okay, Ken you take him around. Rob, I need you to check the south fields. I noticed some of the vines had some kind of fungus on them."

Lindsey saluted and trotted off to the

south. Bell also gave a semi-salute and walked toward the large building behind the machine shed, without waiting for me to follow. Cuthbert gave me one last furrowed brow look, spun on his heels and headed for the inn. That little byplay marked all three of them as former military; a fact I filed away as I turned and followed Bell.

Unlike the mechanical shed, which had single-ply metal sides and a corrugated iron roof, this building had brick walls and a tile roof. In front was a large ten-foot-wide roll-up door, and beside that was a smaller door with a push-button combination lock. Bell went to the small door and punched in a combination. He pulled the door open and stood waiting for me to enter.

I stepped into a room about six feet wide and four feet deep. In front of me was another door with another push-button lock. Bell stepped in behind me and pulled the door closed. As the door lock clicked, lights overhead came on. I looked around at Bell.

"What is this building?" I asked.

He laughed. "Gets everybody the first time," he said. "The co-, er, Mr. Cuthbert, calls it the cellar, even though it doesn't have a cellar. It's where we keep the wine stored. It has to be kept at a constant temperature so it doesn't go sour or something. This room's kinda like an airlock. It keeps the air from outside getting into the cellar."

As he spoke I heard a low hum above me.

In the ceiling, some ten feet above me, were four circular grids, and the flicker of light through the slits indicated the movement of fan blades.

"Sounds like a pretty high-tech operation," I said.

"I guess so." He shrugged. "I don't know jack about the wine making side. I just keep the engines running." He crossed the room, punched in another code and pushed the door open. This time he entered ahead of me and held the door.

The cellar was huge, much larger than it looked from outside. The building was at least fifty feet wide and over one hundred fifty feet deep. It was dimly lit by twelve rectangular light fixtures, in two rows of six suspended from the struts of the ceiling twenty feet above us. Next to each light fixture was a large four-blade fan, lazily turning. Four rows of large wooden casks sitting on top of wooden frame platforms lined the long axis of the building. The walls were rough, unpainted wood plank and the floor was beige stone blocks. Except for the hum and flap of the fan blades, and the whisper of our shoes over the stone floor, the cavernous space was silent.

I whistled. "Wow, this is a lot of wine. How many barrels in here?"

"There's fifty casks, that's what the boss calls 'em, not barrels . . . fifty casks in each row, and each cask holds fifty liters."

"The way we came in, is that the only access to this structure?"

"Yep, and me, Rob and the boss are the only ones with the combination to the two locks."

It didn't seem to make any sense to spend any more time in the building. It was highly unlikely that Leana Sonnenberg would have been able to enter it, or have had any reason to even be near it.

"So, you didn't search this building?"

"We didn't, but when the cops came they insisted on looking. Didn't find anything, though."

"Okay, where else did you search?"

"When Cobane told us the woman was missing, we searched around this area first. We checked the press room and—"

"The press room?"

"That's the building behind here," he said. "It's got the machine that presses the grapes and the mixing vats and stuff. It's kept closed, but it was open that day because the boss was gonna show it to the tour group. Anyway, we looked in there, and so did the cops, but there was no sign of her. After we checked that, we went and looked through the gardens behind the inn, again nada, she was nowhere to be found."

"Show me this press room."

He hesitated, looking over at the machine shed. "Yeah, okay. Boss said show you everything. Come on."

The path from the cellar, a six-foot-wide gravel lane, ran between the cellar and the machine shed. The press room was a quarter the size of the cellar, but similarly constructed. The path split just before reaching it, part making a right angle into a large rectangular space that was also graveled, while the rest kept going straight past the building to connect with what looked like a slightly wider gravel road running east and west.

"What's that road behind the building for?" I asked.

"Oh, that's the road that connects the east and west fields," he said. "The boss doesn't like having us drive service vehicles in front of the inn where guests can see, so we use this back road to move the tractor and work equipment around."

Another bit of information I stored away. My mind when I'm working an investigation is like a file drawer marked 'Miscellaneous.' Every little bit of information that pops up that doesn't fit right away goes there. Later, when I'm synthesizing things, I dip in and start stirring these bits around until a fuller picture starts to form. It's not exactly a scientific process, but it works for me.

"So, can I take a look inside this . . . press room?"

Like the cellar, the press room had a large roll-up door with a smaller door to one side with the same type of push-button lock.

Cuthbert seemed to have a thing for combination locks. I suppose it made sense, though. Limit the number of people with the combination, and you didn't have to worry about lost or stolen keys, and assuming those who had access were part of a trusted inner circle, it made for a pretty secure system.

Bell punched in the numbers and pulled the door open. There was no air lock setup. The door opened into a large room containing a strange looking device on the right, and stacks of empty wine casks on the left. The floor was red brick and covered with dust, except for aa area adjacent to the first stack of casks that looked like something had been dragged across it. Given its location, I assumed this was where they slid the casks to fill them from the press. I pointed at the device, a round wooden tub about six feet in diameter, containing a slit down the near side, and with a large metal tube with flanges suspended in a frame over the center. The device sat atop a circular brick platform about six inches high.

"I take it that's the wine press?"

"Yeah, we bring the grapes in, dump 'em into the tub, and then lower the press in and squeeze the juice out into pans under that slit." He pointed to a work bench in the back of the room. "The other shit that goes into a bottle of wine is added and it's all poured into the casks. When they're full, we bring a forklift over, load 'em onto a wagon and use the tractor to take 'em to the cellar."

He didn't know a whole lot about the wine making process, not that it would have mattered, because I know absolutely nothing about it. What I did know was there were no signs that Leana Sonnenberg had been inside either of the two buildings I'd looked at. That left the garden.

"Let's go look at the garden," I said. "I assume when you did your search, you followed the way she's supposed to have gone?"

"Yeah, and we didn't find a thing."

"How about we go from here by way of that road in back?"

He'd been walking back toward the door, but stopped. I could see the tension in his shoulders, a momentary tightening that he quickly brought under control.

"Sure, if you want to," he said. "But, why?"

"I covered a large part of the path she would have taken, when I walked out to the machine shed, and like you, saw nothing. Maybe by coming at it from a different angle, something might stand out."

He cocked his head and looked at me with a questioning look in his eyes.

"Do all private investigators work like you?"

"I have my own unique methods." I laughed.

"That's for sure," he said. "I never saw a PI on TV work like you."

In all probability there'd never been a PI like me before, and I don't work like the gumshoes you see on TV, no real private investigator does. Mostly we do what I'd just been doing, walk around looking for clues and not finding them, or delivering paperwork.

The rest of our walk around yielded more of the same—nothing. Lindsey, the field manager, never came back, so Bell gave me a quick tour of the nearest areas of the fields that also yielded nothing. I didn't see any point in going any deeper into the rows of grape vines. If Leana had gone there, the best place for evidence would be near the point of entry. The result of checking along the edges of the fields? Nothing. Cuthbert was off somewhere, but I couldn't think of anything else to ask him, so I thanked Bell for being such a patient tour guide. He shrugged, turned away and headed back to his machine shed.

Charles Ray

NINE

On the way back to DC, I stopped and had a pulled pork sandwich at a barbecue joint in a shopping mall north near Gainesville, and then stopped again at the Stone House in Manassas Battlefield Park. After sitting in my car for a few minutes and thinking about the futility of war and how close the country came to being divided if the Confederates had been smart enough to capitalize on their victory in the battles they'd won here, I pulled back onto 29 and headed north.

It was past 2:00 by the time I got back to the office.

"Did you learn anything useful at Brandywine?" Heather asked as soon as I walked in.

"I learned a lot. How much of it will ultimately be useful remains to be seen." While eating my sandwich, I'd scribbled in the notebook I carry with me. I pulled it out of my pocket. "I do have a few things I need you to work your magic on for me."

She took her own notebook out of her desk drawer. My writing is not all that bad, but Heather complains that trying to read it gives her headaches. So, we have two sets of all my notes; mine, which do tend to become unreadable after a few weeks, and hers, that we use for the official case files.

"Someone at Brandywine set off your 'bad guy' alarm?"

Good question. Cobane didn't push any buttons for me, but Cuthbert reminded me of someone, someone I didn't particularly like, and his two henchmen—not sure why, but that's the way I thought of Lindsey and Bell—were worth checking out on general principle.

There was nothing concrete, but my lizard brain was nudging me that Brandywine Estates was central to the case. Leana Sonnenberg went missing from there for one thing, so it had to be the main focus of any search. But, there was something else. Something lurking at the edge of my consciousness that was the answer to all my questions; if only I could think what it was.

"Nothing in particular," I said. "But, since it was from Brandywine that Sonnenberg's wife went missing, we have to check it out thoroughly. I'm particularly interested in the owner, Harlan Cuthbert, and two of his employees, Ken Bell and Hal Lindsey. I think all three are former military, so look into that. While you're at it, check up on Paul Cobane. He's the general manager of the hotel."

She wrote fast, and neat. I have a choice when I write, fast or neat.

"Okay, Cuthbert, Lindsey, Bell, and Cobane. Anything else?"

"Yeah, while you're at it, dig up all you can on Brandywine Estates."

"By all I can, you mean–"

"Everything. Former owners, current debtors, maps of the property, floor plans for the buildings, the works."

"Got it," she said. "I also did some background checking on Jacob and Leana Sonnenberg this morning. Would you like a data dump?"

Does a bear take a crap in the woods? Of course I would, and if she hadn't taken the initiative to do it, I would have asked her to do a background check on the client and the victim; it's just common sense. While I was convinced that Sonnenberg hadn't harmed his wife, it would have been stupid not to double check. After all, more than half the victims of violent crimes in this country are assaulted by a close friend or family member, and when the victim's a wife, the prime suspect is the husband. Over 2,300 women go missing in the U.S. every day, and only about five percent of them are taken by kidnappers unknown to them. In most of the cases, the perpetrator is a husband or boyfriend. With statistics like that, it stands to reason that the cops are going to look at the husband.

I was willing to bet money that the Fauquier County authorities were peeling Sonnenberg's history like an onion. That is, if they even believed that a crime had taken place. My money was on them viewing the whole incident as a young wife running out on her elderly husband.

"Whatcha got?" I asked.

She flipped open her notebook. "Well, you already have the standard bio on them both," she said. "She was, is, 37, and he's 70; not exactly a recipe for a happy marriage in most cases, but from everything I've been able to pick up, they got along well, or as well as two strong-willed people can be expected to get along."

I caught the slight note of hesitancy in her voice.

"There's a 'but' in there somewhere, right?"

"Well, there is one thing." She paused, looking at her notes as if they'd been written by someone else. "Leana Sonnenberg never accompanied her husband on his trips before, preferring to stay here in the area to work on her degree. She wasn't really much of a wine aficionado. According to one of my sources, Sophia McDougall, personal assistant to the editor of the publication he works for, he often asked her to go along, but she always refused . . . until the trip to Brandywine Estates."

"So, you're saying it wasn't his idea for her to accompany him on this trip? He didn't make that clear."

"He's a great writer, but he has a great ego," she said. "I guess he just didn't want to admit that she'd insisted on going on this trip. According to my source, who happened to be visiting their house just before the trip to drop off some papers from the magazine, she was quite insistent about going."

"Did your source say why she insisted on going?"

She shook her head. "No, he just said that after Sonnenberg announced where he was going and why, she said she was going with him."

"What was Sonnenberg's reaction to that?"

"He wasn't too happy. The invitation was for one since she'd refused to accompany him before, and he worried that he'd not be able to make the change in reservations in the time he had before he had to be there. But, she insisted, and finally, he relented. Turned out that Sophie was the one who had to notify Brandywine of the change, and they were most accommodating, so peace was restored, I guess."

I processed that bit of information. The fact that it was Leana's idea to go to Brandywine rather than her husband's was interesting. It further validated my feeling that he hadn't wanted to do her harm, but raised another even more compelling question—why did *she* want to go on this particular trip?—the answer to that question was, I knew deep in my gut, key to what happened.

"So," I said. "The way I see it is, we need to find out why she wanted to go."

"You think there was something about Brandywine that interested her?"

"Either that, or someone at Brandywine." Then I had a thought. "While you're looking into Brandywine and the people there, pay careful attention to any links with Leana; I think her history's the key to this."

She caught my meaning quickly. "While I'm at that, I'll go back and take another look at her background."

"Okay, let me know right away if you find anything," I said. "Right now, I think I'm going home. That was a long drive, and I'm bushed."

TEN

It turned out that I was more exhausted than I thought. After a quick supper and a few minutes of listening to classic music on NPR, Sandra and I hit the sack early. I fell instantly into a dreamless sleep.

My eyes snapped open the next morning, and for a moment I lay there disoriented. I could see no light against the curtains, so I knew it was still dark outside. I looked at my watch on the bedside table. It was 5:30. I turned and saw Sandra peering at me with one eye open.

"You awake, too?" she asked.

"Yeah. Sorry to wake you."

"You didn't. I was actually just lying here waiting for you to wake up. What say we go for an early run?"

Without waiting for my reply, she rolled out of bed and padded into the bathroom. I must have been really wired up and my mood had communicated itself to her. She's usually sound asleep when I wake up, but then, I usually wake up around 6:00. The case, obviously was getting to me, and by extension to her.

I lay there a moment longer, taking in the scent and warmth she left on the bed. Then I rolled off the bed and joined her.

She was just adjusting the strap on her sports bra when I entered and grabbed my sweats off the hook on the door. We pulled on our sweat bottoms at the same time, although I have to confess that the sight of her pulling wrinkled gray sweat pants over exquisitely shaped legs and to-die-for hips is far more pleasant than watching my grimy sweats enclose muscular but scarred legs and a butt that's starting to lose some of its firmness. I paused in pulling on my sweat shirt to watch her raise her arms to pull hers over her blonde hair, now pulled into a pony tail, and down over breasts that would turn heads in a monastery.

"Damn," I said as she tugged on the hem of the shirt to adjust it. "My heart rate's already up just watching you do that."

She stuck her tongue out at me. "Let's see if we can get it higher when you watch my ass move as I leave you in the dust," she said.

Now, that is guaranteed to pull my dirty mind back down to earth. Next to puzzles, the next thing I can't resist is a challenge.

"So, it's not just a pleasant jog this morning, eh? You want a race, lady, you got it. From the porch and back, loser does dishes for a week."

"You're on," she said, and squeezed past me.

I followed, watching the sway of her hips. Who would have ever thought that gray sweat pants could be so sexy? I thought for a brief, mad moment that it might be worth doing dishes alone for a week just to watch that for four miles. Like hell. I've never thrown a contest in my life, not even for that.

Outside we stood at the foot of the back porch steps, side by side.

"Okay, the usual course," I said. "No short cuts, and no tripping or bumping."

She was all business now. Sandra thrives on a challenge as much as I do. She placed her left foot two feet forward and bent slightly forward at the waist, a look of determination on her face.

"On my mark," she said. "Ready, set, . . . go!"

She kicked off to a strong start a heartbeat before she said 'go,' gaining five yards on me in her first three strides because I started flatfooted instead of pushing off with my strong foot. It didn't matter in the end, though. I have the greater lung capacity and the stronger leg muscles, and after a mile of watching her gluteus maximus muscles undulate, I put on a burst of speed and zipped past her. I maintained the lead for the next mile out and back, easing off a few yards from the porch steps, allowing her to get close enough behind me that I could hear her breathing.

I turned, running in place, and waited for her to pull up in front of me. We both spent a few minutes running in place to cool down. Our breathing calmed about the same time.

"Want to join me in meditation this morning?" I asked.

"Sounds like a good idea," she said.

We arranged ourselves side by side on the edge of the porch, facing the forest. When Sandra and I first started seeing each other she'd happened upon me meditating and expressed an interest. Along with teaching her martial arts, I'd been showing her the meditation techniques taught to me by the old Korean who also taught me taekwondo and a modified form of kungfu. She took to mediation *and* martial arts like a calf to its mother's teat.

We didn't do the 'ah-oom' chanting that so many get into. My teacher had taught me to find your proper balance within yourself by simply relaxing and letting your mind and body come into harmony with each other and your surroundings. There's no going into a trancelike state, or shutting off the outside world. On the contrary, you let the outside world *in*; you merely pay it no special mind. Instead of *listening* for sounds, you allow yourself to *hear* the sounds that are all around you, and that are often ignored. You don't *look* for things, you *see* them. The gemlike appearance of dust motes as the early morning sunlight hits them, the whispering of a gentle breeze as it slides across lush green leaves. You *feel* the blood coursing through your veins and the air as it flows into and out of your nose.

A few minutes of this each day helped purge my body and mind of the previous day's toxins, and enhanced the benefits of sleep and exercise. It also enhances my ability to sense and appreciate my surroundings.

As if we were in tune with each other, Sandra and I raised our hands, rotating them from palm up to palm down, at the same time, inhaled deeply, and slowly let it out.

"Wow," she said. "I wish I'd known how to do this in college. It would have helped ease the stress of many an exam."

I knew how she felt. Before I was taught to meditate—actually, my Korean *paksa* would have said 'learned' because, he often said, some things cannot be taught, the student must learn them on his own—I was as tightly wound as a violin string, and was a prime candidate for an ulcer before thirty. Meditation taught me to see and appreciate the world, and to take everything easy and in stride. The fact that it was taught to me by a Korean, a man from one of the most volatile races in Asia, if not the world, is never lost on me. Unlike most of the other Koreans I met during my army time in the 'Frozen Chosin,' who seemed incapable of quiet or restrained speech and were forever arguing about something, Mr. Suh was the epitome of calm, and not once during the two years I studied with him did I ever hear him raise his voice or appear angry.

I was about to make some smart ass comment in response to what she'd said when a flash of brown in the edge of the forest caught my eye. She saw it about the same time, and pointed.

"Is that—"

"Yeah, it's a whitetail doe and a fawn," I said. Then, I saw something I'd never seen before. "No, two fawns."

Her intake of breath was loud in my ears.

"My goodness, is that a calf following deer?"

"No," I said. "You're seeing something that's extremely rare. That white animal with the small patches of brown is a piebald whitetail fawn."

She leaned forward, her eyes round like saucers. "You're kidding! I've never seen a deer with that coloration before."

"It's only the second one I've ever seen. They're extremely rare. I read somewhere that only one in every hundred deer born is piebald, less than one percent of the total deer population."

"What causes it, some kind of intermixing with some other animal?"

"No, it's some kind of genetic aberration." I watched the doe and the two fawns as they moved slowly out of the tree line and the doe began nibbling at the grass in the open area while the two fawns went for her engorged teats.

The first one still had the white dots in its fur. The piebald, almost completely white except for six or eight brown patches the size of my head, was showing two small bumps on its forehead, indicating that it was male. Brother and sister, they playfully jostled each other as they sucked. Every now and then, the doe would raise her head from the grass and look at them.

"It's beautiful," she said. "They all are, but that one's especially striking. Why are you looking so sad?"

"I agree it's beautiful, but I also read that they're usually born with deformities, like overbites or undersized lungs, and they seldom survive past the first year."

Her face contorted into a frown and her lips quivered. She looked at me with an expression of immense sadness. "Such a beautiful creature. Sometimes I wonder about a world where such things can happen."

"Even worse than the fact that they're born with physical limitations that make it hard for them to survive, that beautiful coloration makes them easier targets for predators than the normal deer; that, and there are hunters who like to take them because they *are* so rare. It makes a trophy to brag about."

She shuddered and wrapped her arms around her body.

There was nothing more either of us could say, so we just sat there watching the three deer until they wandered back into the dark shadows of the forest, leaving me sitting there thinking just how fleeting beauty is.

ELEVEN

Heather was sitting at her desk, facing the door when I walked into the office. She had her notebook open on her lap, and that 'I got something you might find interesting' look on her face.

"Can I get my second cup of coffee before you do your data dump?" I said, sweeping past her and going into my office.

We'd once kept the coffee maker on the cabinet in her part of the office, but she doesn't drink coffee, so I felt it unfair to subject her to the smell—aroma to me—of coffee all day, so I moved the coffee maker to the top of the bookcase in my office.

I took the pot out to our common bathroom, a unisex broom closet with a commode and wash basin in the far corner of Heather's office, and filled it. Back in my office, I measured out two tablespoons of Jamaican blend and dumped them into the filter in the top of the coffee maker. I pushed the switch to on, and, with nothing better to do, stood there and watched as it first hissed, then bubbled, and finally dripped coffee from the reservoir on top, down through the filter and into the six-cup pot. I poured myself a mug, sniffed appreciatively at it, took a sip, and was at last ready to absorb Heather's information.

She hadn't moved in the time it took me to get that first of sip of coffee down my gullet. When I walked back out and straddled the chair next to her desk, she placed her notebook on the desk and fixed me with an icy stare. "Is your brain working now?" she asked.

I took another sip of coffee.

"Like a steel trap ready to spring," I said. I put my mug on the edge of the desk and folded my arms on the back of the chair. "What nuggets of wisdom do you wish to impart, oh great teacher?"

Ignoring my jibe, she looked down at her notebook. "Just keep in mind, though, that this is unconfirmed information. It came second and third hand, so take it for what it's worth."

"Hey, kiddo, I'll take your second-hand information over first hand from most people any day, so shoot."

"Okay, first we'll do Leana Sonnenberg, or as she was known at the time, Staff Sergeant Leana Colman to my source. She did a tour of duty at Fort Meade, Maryland as a truck driver, which was her army specialty, and then was transferred south to Fort Belvoir in Virginia. Down there she was transferred from the supply unit to a special transportation unit on the base that ferried VIPs around; VIPs being the officers with rank of lieutenant colonel and above, and a few high level civilians. The word is that she was thinking of reenlisting, and that she was up for promotion to Sergeant First Class, whatever that is."

"That's a pretty high rank for a mere driver," I said. "She must have been driving for some pretty heavy hitters."

"She was. Apparently she was chauffer for a lot of colonels who dealt with contractors, and high ranking contractors who did business with the base." She ran her finger down the page. "My source said she was also being considered for officer training, which was unusual for someone her age, but she got pretty high ratings from the people she worked for, so they were pulling strings to get her commissioned. Anyway, the source said that one day she just walked into the headquarters and informed them that she wasn't going to reenlist and that she was leaving the army."

"Did your source tell you why?"

"No, he didn't know," she said. "The scuttlebutt was that she'd had some kind of run-in with one of her passengers, a colonel who worked closely with some of the contractors, but my source said he could never pin it down. Anyway, when her tour ended, she packed up and left. Went back to Baltimore where she got a job driving for a limo company. Another source from up there told me she was doing a pretty good job, but she seemed to be a bit sad and distracted at first. Except for her sister she didn't really socialize much; actually, this source said she didn't socialize at all. Just worked and went home after her shifts or to classes at the college where she was enrolled. Apparently, though, one of her customers was impressed enough with her that when she drove him to a wine tasting, he invited her to park the limo and accompany him inside to the event. That's where she met Jacob Sonnenberg. The two of them, for reasons no one understands, hit it off, and were soon an item. After a short courtship, they got married, and she moved to DC and enrolled in school down here."

It was in interesting story, but I couldn't see how it related to her going missing.

"I'll file all that away," I said. "But, I'm not sure how it'll help me find her."

She flipped a few more pages. "I'm not sure either, but that's what I found." I could tell the way she paused her finger over the page, though, that she wasn't done yet. "There is one other thing, though, that I thought you'd find especially interesting."

She paused. I tensed up. When Heather

doles out information in fragments like this, I know she's got something that's more than *interesting*. She's hit a tidbit that is *hot*. She just likes to string me along sometimes.

"Okay, I'm waiting."

"I started looking up this guy, Harlan Cuthbert, like you asked, and you'll never guess where he worked before he bought Brandywine Estates."

"Baltimore?" That, of course, would be too much to ask for.

"No, not even close. Cuthbert was in the army. He retired a year or so ago, and bought the place . . . for cash. He was a colonel with thirty years in when he checked out. Now, I don't know how much money a colonel makes, or how much he saved in thirty years, but that place cost him five million dollars, and that's just the land and buildings that were already there. Since buying it, he's sunk a few more million into renovating the inn and installing the winemaking equipment."

Again, interesting, but she wasn't done. As usual, she saved the best for last.

"His last assignment before he retired was with some kind of test and development outfit at Fort Belvoir. He was primary liaison with some of the main contractors." She paused for effect. "And, he was there at the same time as Leana Colman."

I had an 'ah ha!' moment. I *knew* that Cuthbert had a military background. There was something about the way he carried himself that marked him as clearly as a painted sign hanging around his neck. But, what I hadn't figured on was a connection to the missing woman. It wasn't coming together completely in my mind, but the outlines were there.

"So, there's a good chance that they knew each other," I said. "Maybe Cuthbert was even one of her passengers when she was a driver there."

"That's what I thought. But, it still doesn't get us any closer to what happened to her."

"No, but it's a trail that needs to be followed. Keep digging on Cuthbert, and while you're at it, don't forget Bell and Lindsey. I'll bet they're former soldiers and it wouldn't surprise me to learn they were at Belvoir at the same time as Leana and Cuthbert. In the meantime, I think I need to pay our client a visit."

TWELVE

Jacob Sonnenberg's house was in a ritzy section of town north of Georgetown University, on Davis Street, northwest of the vice president's residence at the U.S. Naval Observatory. There were six houses in his block, three on each side of the street. In less affluent areas of the city, a block that long would have at least eight, but the rich don't like to be crowded. I'm not rich, but I can relate to that, which is why I live where I do.

His house was the middle one on the right, a two-story red brick colonial with a black tile roof and a white-fronted entryway that was flanked by two large evergreens in expensive looking blue Chinese vases. He had a two-car garage with a low hedge bordering the driveway, and a cobblestone walkway from the driveway to the front. Small circular beds with red, yellow, and purple flowers ran in a zig-zag pattern from the house to the sidewalk, and his lawn was manicured to a fare the well.

I pulled into the driveway, got out and walked to the door. The doorbell sounded like chimes in some fancy cathedral. I expected a maid in costume or a butler in livery to answer the door, but Sonnenberg himself opened it. He had a hang dog look on his face, but his eyes widened in surprise when he saw me.

"Uh, Mr. Pennyback, please come in." He stepped aside for me to enter. "I hope you have some positive news, I could really use some right about now."

"I wish I had some good news for you, in fact, any news," I said. "But, we're a bit stuck right now. I went to Brandywine and had a look myself, but unfortunately, I came up as dry as the police did."

He followed me through a wide entrance hall lined with smaller copies of the Chinese vases outside with expensive looking original watercolor paintings on the floral patterned walls into a sunken living room furnished in American colonial style, with more vases and a couple of bronze horses on separate stands, and oil paintings arranged in tasteful groupings on all but the side wall, which was mostly a large picture window that looked out on a miniature English garden that was a maze of privet hedges encircling a square pebble surface containing a marble backless bench.

He motioned me toward a large sofa with fluffy cushions and lace doilies on the arms and back.

"If you have no news, why are you here?"

"I find myself in need of more information," I said. "I've been trying to determine who might have had reason to harm your wife, but in order to do that I need to know more about her."

"What more can I tell you? I've told you that she had few friends here, other than her . . . sister. Certainly no one who would want to hurt her."

His hesitation when he mentioned Laura sent my mind off on a momentary tangent.

"You and Laura Colman don't seem to get along. Why is that?"

"Would you like a cup of tea or coffee, Mr. Pennyback?"

This was a question he seemed hesitant to answer, but I didn't think pressuring him was a good idea.

"Coffee would be fine."

"I have a pot on in the kitchen," he said. "If you'd like, we can talk in the breakfast nook, so the coffee pot's conveniently located. I don't like moving it around."

He walked out of the pit that was the living room's main area, past the large picture window, and through a door. I rose and followed. We passed through a large formal dining room that had a table and twelve chairs and a large buffet sideboard done in rich, dark brown wood. A gigantic crystal chandelier hung over the center of the table was glistening and twinkling as the light from the window over the sideboard struck it. Through a doorless archway we entered the kitchen, a room as large as half my house, with gleaming modern appliances, including a walk-in freezer. The breakfast nook was tucked into the right corner; a small round table and four chairs. The table was covered by a red and white checkered table cloth. A simple glass vase containing one red rose sat in the center of the table. The chairs were standard wooden chairs of the kind you buy at your local furniture discount warehouse. I stopped and stared.

"Quite different from the rest of the house, right?" he asked, as if reading my mind. "I know what you're thinking. After seeing the rest of the house, this cozy little nook is so out of character. It was Leana's idea. She said that when the two of us had meals in the dining room it was too much like eating in an army mess hall. I have no idea what that's like, but if this is what made her feel good, it was fine with me. Funny thing, after a few weeks, I found I preferred it here as well. We only ever use the dining room when we have guests, and that's really a rare event. Have a seat, and I'll get us coffee. I imagine you take yours black."

I nodded and took a chair giving me a good view of the kitchen. When the coffee maker stopped spewing brown liquid into the pot, he took two plain white ceramic mugs from the cabinet over the sink and filled them. He took the chair opposite me and pushed one of the mugs my way. Then, he lifted his mug and blew on it for a while, staring down at the steam rising from the surface. After taking a tentative sip, he put the mug down and propped his elbows on the table, looking across at me with a sad expression.

"It's true what you say. Laura and I don't exactly get along. But, it's . . . well, in a way, it is probably as much my fault as hers I suppose." He lifted the mug and took another sip. I lifted my own and sipped. It was rich, heady Jamaican coffee, brewed strong, just the way I like it. I put my mug down and sat there with as much of a neutral expression as I could manage, waiting him out. Finally, he sighed heavily. "It's probably *all* my fault really. I never stopped to try and see things from her perspective. Leana was more than a sister to her, you know. After their parents were killed, Leana became a mother as well. I suppose, looking back on it, I should have expected Laura to resent me taking her mother away from her, and done more to ease the situation."

It made sense, as far as it went, but I wanted the full story. "She told me that you tried to keep Leana from spending time with her."

He looked at me as he played with his mug. There was pain in his eyes. "Yes, I suppose in a childish fit of pique I did do that," he said. "In some ways I'm no different from Laura. I resent anyone who competes with me for Leana's attention." He shrugged as he said it.

I couldn't help but laugh. "So, this is just a major case of sibling rivalry gone out of control, except that it's you and Laura acting like feuding siblings."

Some of the tension went out of his face in response to my lame attempt at humor. "Yes, I guess that's what it is. You'd think a seventy-year-old with three masters' degrees would be above all that, wouldn't you?"

"The heart wants what the heart wants, and the rest of the body just tags along for the ride, no matter the age," I said. "Look, that explains one little thing that was bothering me, but it's not really why I came here to talk to you."

"You want to know more about Leana, but I really don't know what I can tell you that I already haven't told you, or that you can't find through your investigation."

"I have a feeling that Leana's disappearance is somehow connected to her time in the military," I said. "What do you know about that period of her life?"

He looked confused. "I don't understand. What would her military service have to do with any of this?"

"Right now, it's just a feeling I have, and I don't want to prejudice your recollections. What do you know about her time in the army?"

"Not much I'm afraid." He rubbed his chin. "Leana didn't like talking about it. She was in Iraq during the first Gulf War, you know, and I imagine she saw a lot of things that she'd rather forget. I suspect she might have been suffering from post-traumatic stress, but Leana's such a strong-willed woman, she would never ask anyone else for help. She'd just deal with it on her own."

Not the smartest idea in the world, but I could relate. I'd had a minor bout of PTSD, post-traumatic stress disorder, after my first mission involving a fire fight, and some serious issues after a mission in Somalia when our target, a particularly vicious war lord, had his family in the target area, and we'd been forced to take them all out. I dealt with each issue on my own when I recognized them. But, when Sara and Ethan were killed, I fell apart. If not for my friend Buster Mayweather being there for me, I might not have recovered.

"I'm more interested in her time after Iraq," I said. "She was stationed in this area, first up at Fort Meade, and just before she left the army she was assigned to a transportation unit at Fort Belvoir, Virginia. Did you know that?"

"Yes, but not the details." He closed his

Charles Ray

eyes and furrowed his brow. "Now that you mention that, she seemed more reluctant to talk about that period, especially her time in Fort Belvoir, than she did to talk about the war. You think her assignment at one of those places might have something to do with this? I know they have that super-secret government agency up there in Maryland, but surely they don't go around kidnapping Americans. I mean, she was just a driver, she couldn't have been involved in anything that sensitive . . . could she?"

I didn't think it would make him feel better to know that if the stakes were high enough, that very thing could happen. But, I also didn't think this case had anything to do with intelligence operations.

"My gut tells me that there's the likelihood that something or someone from her last assignment is involved in whatever happened."

His hands trembled as he clasped them around the mug. There was pain in his expression.

"Tell me bluntly, Mr. Pennyback," he said. "Do you think Leana's still alive?"

That was a good question, one that I didn't have a logical answer to. Deep in my gut I knew that she was alive, but I couldn't tell anyone why. Hell, I wasn't even sure myself. I'm not a believer in the occult or anything like that, but I do think that there's a part of our brain that knows things that the logical parts don't necessarily have ready access to. I also knew that I was looking at a man nearing the end of his tether. I wasn't about to sever the last string of hope he had.

"Yeah, I think she's still alive," I said. "And, I damn well intend to find her."

His gaze bored into me, and I guess he saw that I was being straight with him. He sighed. "Good. I hope you're right, I really do. I don't know what I'd do if she . . ."

"Don't worry. I'll find her. You got my word on that."

He smiled weakly. The phone rang. The warbling sound coming from the instrument, one of those cordless phones that sits in a little charging cradle, caused his to flinch.

After four rings, he rose wearily and crossed the kitchen to the counter and picked up the phone.

"Hello," he said.

His brow furrowed as he listened to the person on the other end of the line.

"Is that really necessary?" he asked.

A look of worry, bordering on panic, creased his face.

"I see." He put his hand over the phone's mouthpiece. "It's the police," he said barely above a whisper. "The Fauquier County authorities want to talk to me about my wife's case, and it didn't sound like it was an invitation."

That was something I'd been worried about. The police always look at the spouse first, but I'd been hoping that with the lack of evidence in this case, it'd be a while before they started putting pressure on Sonnenberg.

He could always refuse to talk to them, but that would only make it look like he was hiding something. On the other hand, no private citizen should go into a meeting with the police that could potentially lead to charges, and was definitely based on suspicion, without professional help.

"Did they ask you to come anywhere?" I asked.

"No, they want to come here."

Slick, I thought. Interview the 'suspect' on familiar ground, put him at ease, and hope he'll slip up.

"Okay, tell them two hours," I said.

"Can you come in two hours?" he asked into the phone. "Do you need directions? Oh, I see, very well then."

He hung up.

"Now," I said. "Call your lawyer."

THIRTEEN

I had assumed that Quincy Chang would be Sonnenberg's lawyer for everything, and had been right. My old army buddy arrived within forty-five minutes of being called. He walked into the sunken living room, looking ready for the courtroom in his light gray suit, cream colored shirt, and red power tie. And, he came to do business.

"Fill me in," he said as soon as we were all seated around the coffee table with mugs of coffee close at hand.

Sonnenberg did.

"I have no idea what's put the burr under their saddle," I said. "Unless they have some new evidence that we're not privy to, there's nothing to really indicate foul play."

"Then, we'll play it by ear. Don't answer any question other than your name without looking at me first," he told Sonnenberg. "Let's see if we can get them to show their cards." He looked over at me. "As for you, Al, I think that unless they ask you a direct question it's best if you just observe and say nothing."

That made sense to me. The police are never happy about a private investigator sticking a finger in their business. Sonnenberg wouldn't be looking all that good in their eyes, having his lawyer present, and I would only be adding fire to the flame if I poked my nose in unless invited, so I nodded my acceptance of Quincy's advice. It wouldn't be easy, though. I have a hard time sitting idly by when someone's being bullied, and I had a feeling that at some point that's exactly what they'd do.

"Now, Jacob," Quincy said. "Why don't you fill me in on what happened at Brandywine. I know you told me before, but it wouldn't hurt to refresh my memory."

Sonnenberg went back over the events leading up to his wife not returning to their suite, speaking in a monotone. He was like a man just waking up from a coma. The strain as he remembered the event was plain on his face. He'd just finished his story when the doorbell rang.

Quincy stood and started for the door, but Sonnenberg held up a hand. "It'll probably be better if I get it," he said. "You'll be a shock enough for them without yours being the first face they see."

"Good idea," Quincy said, sitting back down.

Sonnenberg went to the front door. He returned a few moments later with Buster Mayweather and two people, a man and a woman, in civilian dress. Buster's eyes widened when he saw me, and got a curious look on it when his gaze landed on Quincy.

The two behind him took in the scene with frowns. Sonnenberg pointed them to another sofa, a twin of the one Quincy and I sat on. "Please have a seat and introduce yourselves," he said. "Can I offer you coffee?"

Buster stepped aside and let his companions go first to the sofa. "No thanks," he said. "I'm hoping we won't be here long." He still looked curiously at me. "I'm Detective First Class Buster Mayweather from the DC Metropolitan Police. My colleagues are Sheriff's Deputies Andrew Mansfield and Christina Fontaine from the Fauquier County Sheriff's Office. They've been assigned to investigate your wife's disappearance, Mr. Sonnenberg, and have requested my department's assistance in interviewing you." He nodded at the two.

Mansfield, a square jawed man of middle years, with watery blue eyes, five o'clock shadow, and close cropped brown hair, took a leather folder from his jacket and held it up so that Sonnenberg could see his badge. His partner, a tall woman who looked to be in her early thirties, with wide hips, large breasts and blonde hair that hung straight down to just below her ears, did the same.

"Mr. Sonnenberg," Mansfield said. "Deputy Fontaine and I just need to ask you a few questions to help us properly investigate your wife's case. Given your . . . prominence in the area, we decided it would be better to talk to you here rather than ask you to come to our office. Since it's outside our jurisdiction, Detective Mayweather was assigned to accompany us." As he spoke, he kept a steely gaze on Quincy and me.

Sonnenberg looked at Quincy who nodded. "I'm happy to answer any questions that I can, deputy." He inclined his head toward Quincy. "Mr. Quincy Chang here is my attorney, though, so for the most part, *he* will be the one answering your questions."

"This is just a routine interview, sir," Mansfield said. "There's really no need to have a lawyer present."

Sonnenberg sat down next to Quincy.

"My client understands that," Quincy said before Sonnenberg could respond. "But, when he informed me that you were coming, I felt it best to be here, so that there would be no chance of anything being misunderstood."

The two county cops looked at Quincy; Mansfield with a look of displeasure, Fontaine with an appraising eye. That didn't surprise me too much. Quincy, a third generation Chinese-American is as tall as me, with a slender build from working out and sailing, and he's been known to turn a few female heads. He had his lawyer face on, but I could tell from the angle of his head that he was checking her out as well, but not being too obvious about it.

After a few seconds, Mansfield's gaze slid from Quincy to me. His thick brows arched upwards a fraction of an inch. "And, you are?"

"This is Mr. Al Pennyback," Quincy said quickly. "He's a private investigator on retainer by my firm."

Fontaine shifted her gaze from Quincy to me. She didn't look like she was appraising me; at least, not in the way she'd been appraising Quincy. I got a feeling that she didn't like PIs very much.

Mansfield took a small tape recorder from his jacket pocket. "Do you have any objection to me recording this interview?"

Quincy took an even smaller recorder from the pocket of his impeccably tailored jacket. "Not at all," he said. "In fact, I'll be making a recording as well."

Mansfield put his recorder on the coffee table and slid it toward Sonnenberg. Quincy put his on the table next to Mansfield's.

Both Mansfield and Fontaine looked like they'd just had sudden attacks of indigestion. Buster, who'd taken a seat next to them, smiled.

"Hey, Al," he said. "Long time, no see."

"You know Mr. Pennyback?" Mansfield asked.

"Yeah, Al and I go way back. He's one of the . . . no, he's *the* top private dick in DC. We've worked together a time or two. He's good people."

Their hostile looks eased—a little. There's nothing like getting an endorsement from another cop to smooth the way. But, they weren't completely convinced. Fontaine kept giving me the look.

"Okay, Mr. Sonnenberg," Mansfield said. "I know you gave a statement to the officer who answered the call at Brandywine, but would you mine just going over what happened the day your wife disappeared?"

Sonnenberg looked at Quincy. Quincy nodded. He related pretty much the same story he'd told me. He kept his composure until he got to the part about waking up and discovering that Leana was not there. By the time he got to the part about the first search by the estate staff finding no trace of her, he was pausing after every few words and taking deep breaths. His voice had become hoarse.

When he finished, he took a deep breath and sat back looking up at the ceiling. "Have you found anything? Anything at all?" he asked.

"No, I'm sorry, sir," Fontaine said. "But, we've gone over the estate twice, and can find nothing indicating your wife was ever there, other than your statement and that of the staff at the inn."

Mansfield snapped his fingers and glared at me. "Pennyback! I thought your name sounded familiar. You were nosing around Brandywine Estates the other day. You mind telling me why you were there?"

My gut instinct was to tell him to piss off because it was none of his business, but that wasn't exactly the truth, and besides, it wouldn't help Sonnenberg.

"I was hired to look into Mrs. Sonnenberg's disappearance," I said.

Buster's smile got wider, and he got that knowing look in his eyes that I've seen him get when we've worked together and we have an evil-doer in a corner; a satisfied look of a predator who has finally run his prey into a corner from which he cannot escape. It's a look he gets when he has some gang banger up against a wall with no alibi, or when he sees an officious fellow cop about to get his comeuppance. Alas, to keep from putting Sonnenberg in a more difficult situation that he was already in, it wouldn't be me administering that comeuppance.

"Why did you feel the need to hire a private investigator, Mr. Sonnenberg?" Fontaine asked.

"Tell me, deputies," Quincy said. "Have you *any* leads on Mrs. Sonnenberg's whereabouts or her condition?" He asked the question in a monotone and kept a deadpan expression on his face.

Red spots blossomed on their cheeks. "Uh, well no," Mansfield said. "But, we're putting every resource we can spare into this case."

"But, the bottom line is, you have nothing." Quincy's voice now had steel in it. "Mr. Sonnenberg hired Mr. Pennyback on my recommendation. Has Mr. Pennyback interfered with your investigation in any way?"

At Holcombe, Stein and Chang, the law firm where Quincy is a partner, they don't do much trial work, and no criminal cases, but Quincy had been an army JAG lawyer for over a decade before getting out of the army and going into private practice. He had a lot of practice facing down colonels in courts martial, so two county mounties didn't stand a chance against him when he put his courtroom face on. And, boy did he have his courtroom face on.

"Well, no he hasn't interfered . . . yet," Mansfield conceded. "We were just curious."

"Al's had a lot of experience working with the police," Buster said. "I can guarantee you he won't get in your way. Matter of fact, he's likely to find things you guys might miss." They scowled at him. He held his hands up, palms out. "No insult intended, guys, that's just the way it is."

I can always depend on Buster to have my back. He's been there for me since the night my wife and son were wiped out in a traffic accident. In fact, it was with cops from

Virginia that time as well. He'd escorted them to notify me of the accident, had gone with me to the morgue to identify the bodies, and stayed with me for hours while I grieved. We've been friends since.

"Just to keep you folks in the loop, I found nothing either," I said.

"You'll keep us informed if you do find anything," Mansfield said. It wasn't a question. He took a name card from his wallet and tossed it across the table toward me. "You can reach me at that number any time, day or night."

Quincy shook his head slightly without looking at me. I didn't need him to speak to know he didn't want me answering that question. At the same time, I also knew he wouldn't want me upsetting them, so I just looked blankly at Mansfield and kept my mouth shut.

Mansfield frowned, and looked from me to Sonnenberg. "Now, Mr. Sonnenberg, just a few more questions if you don't mind." Sonnenberg shrugged. "You and your wife had an argument just before she disappeared, is that correct?"

Quincy's eyes narrowed, but he nodded.

"Yes, we did," Sonnenberg said. "I didn't think it was a good idea for her to get sunburned or dusty walking through the vineyard. We were scheduled to attend a reception that night, and I wanted her to look her best."

"Did you two argue often?" Fontaine asked.

Again, Quincy nodded.

"No more than any other couple, I suppose. My wife and I are both strong-willed people, and we both have . . . artistic temperaments, so we disagree on a number of things. But, we both also respect each other's views, so our disagreements never last for long."

"If you invited your wife to go along with you on this trip, why would you object to her doing something she enjoyed?" Fontaine asked.

"You don't have to answer that," Quincy said.

"No, Quincy, I'd like to. First of all, deputy, I didn't invite Leana to come, she insisted on coming, and secondly, my wife was in the army for a long time. She hated hiking, camping or being outdoors unless she was driving. She didn't even like picnics."

"If she didn't like the outdoors, why would she want to go on a tour of a vineyard?" Mansfield asked.

I wondered if the two of them rehearsed the technique of alternating with questions as a way of throwing interviewees off. It kept Sonnenberg's head swiveling from side to side. I'd have to talk to Heather about including the technique in our investigations some time.

"I really have no idea, deputy," he said.

"No idea at all. I'm not even sure why she wanted to go with me on this trip. When we were first married, I invited her to go along on all my trips, but she always said no."

"What was so special about this trip?" Fontaine asked.

"I have no idea, deputy; no idea at all."

I was willing to bet he'd pass a polygraph, but the looks of skepticism on their faces said that Mansfield and Fontaine weren't buying it. I knew the looks. Despite having no corpse, or even a hint that a murder had been committed, they'd come to a conclusion in their minds that it had, and worse, that Sonnenberg was the killer, so nothing he said was going to change their minds. In fact, they would interpret everything he said as just another sign of guilt.

"Mr. Sonnenberg, do you know anyone who might want to hurt your wife?" Mansfield leaned forward as he spoke. He tried to look sympathetic, but the lack of sincerity in his question was as clear to me as a six-foot high neon sign. He was just trying to put Sonnenberg at ease, hoping to trip him up later on. "Or anyone who might want to hurt you by kidnapping her?"

"No. I mean, a lot of vineyards haven't been exactly pleased with the reviews I've written over the years, but I can't see them going to such an extent to get revenge for a bad review."

Now, Fontaine leaned forward. "Mr.

Sonnenberg, do you have an insurance policy on your wife?" Hah! I'd seen that coming. Good cop, bad cop. The look of shock on Sonnenberg's face, though, showed that it was an effective maneuver. Fortunately, Quincy's as quick as me.

He laid a hand on Sonnenberg's arm, and speared Fontaine with a frosty stare. "You mind explaining the relevancy of that question, deputy?"

She pulled back, eyes wide.

"Hold your water, counselor," she said. "I'm just curious is all."

"Well, if it has nothing to do with the case at hand, I would advise you to stick to relevant questions. My client doesn't have the time to indulge your idle curiosity."

"It might be more than just curiosity," Mansfield said. "It could be relevant to Mrs. Sonnenberg's disappearance."

"Relevant, relevant in what way?"

Quincy's question was rhetorical. Even I knew why they were focusing on that information. If Sonnenberg had a big life insurance policy on his wife, it could be a motive for him to do her in. From the looks on their faces, though, it seems that was all they had; not enough to arrest him, just another piece of the puzzle. Quincy's resistance was unexpected. Hell, his presence had caught them off guard. They shared a look.

"Forget it, counselor," Mansfield said. "Mr.

Sonnenberg, we might have a few additional questions for you. Next time, though, it'll be at our office in Warrenton."

It was a threat, and it wasn't lost on Quincy, but he wasn't intimidated.

"If you wish to speak with Mr. Sonnenberg," he said. "You will call me." He took a silver card case from his inside coat pocket and withdrew one of his engraved name cards. "And, I will arrange to escort him to your offices."

They both looked like they wanted to resist. The law, though, had them by the short and curly—well, had Mansfield by the short and curly; I imagine Fontaine was feeling pinched somewhere else from the look on her face—now that Sonnenberg had involved his attorney, unless they decided to arrest him, or even if they did, they had to deal with said attorney. I wasn't sure what kind of lawyers they were accustomed to dealing with in Fauquier County, but it was clear that they looked upon Quincy as a shark, and they had to be feeling like chum in the water. I couldn't restrain a smile, which earned me a glare from Buster, but I could see the corners of his mouth twitching in a suppressed smile, so I ignored him.

The two deputies stood. There was really little else that could be said. They'd played a long shot and come up empty. It didn't mean they were completely beaten, though. The stony set of their faces said they'd just begun to fight. Now, they'd redouble their efforts to pin *something* on Jacob Sonnenberg. That put the pressure on me to find his wife, and find her soon.

"Okay, guys," Buster said to them. "I'll meet you outside at the car. I need to have a few words with my friends."

Their eyes narrowed, and Fontaine opened her mouth to say something, but Mansfield put a hand on her arm. He hadn't missed that Buster had said 'friends' instead of 'friend,' and he had to be wondering who, besides me, he was referring to. Wisely, though, he wasn't going to push it. He and his partner were out of their jurisdiction; here in DC they were just a pair of civilians with licenses to carry guns—something not many civilians in the District have—and furthermore, Buster Mayweather, a former college football player who still works out and can bench press 250 pounds, is not someone you want to get confrontational with.

"Sure, detective," he said.

After they were gone, Buster stood at the top of the steps leading down into the sunken living room.

"Al, Quincy, I hope you dudes know what you're doing," he said. "Those two were pretty tight lipped, but I know they think your client did something to his wife." He shot a glance at Sonnenberg who was sitting on the sofa looking dazed. "They just don't have enough proof to haul him in."

That was pretty obvious. "But, they don't even know what happened to her, or where she is," I said.

"Hey, she's been missing for nearly two weeks and there's been no ransom note, so it's a pretty good bet she wasn't kidnapped. They can't rule out that she just up and ran off, but my gut tells me they think she's been killed and body's been stashed somewhere."

"Yeah, but without a body, how do they expect to get an arrest warrant, much less an indictment or conviction?"

"Well," Quincy said. "That's not exactly true. If they have enough evidence, even circumstantial, of foul play, they could prosecute, and might even be able to get a conviction. A couple years ago, a guy in Seattle was convicted of killing his wife in 1990, even though her body was never found. Even though they didn't have a body, a weapon, or a witness to the crime, the guy got 60 years in prison for first degree murder. And, back in 1969, a truck driver in New Jersey was convicted of killing a teenage hitchhiker even though her body was never found. And, those are just the two cases I can remember off the top of my head. In law school there were others that were mentioned in some of my classes, going all the way back to the 1800s. Last, but not least, amigo, we're talking about a fucking rural Virginia county. The sheriff down there's an elected official, and I bet you his ass is on the hot seat to close this case. You know how these rural dudes can be; they're a close knit bunch. They like to keep their shit all sewed up tight. If they want your man to go down for killing his wife, they won't stop until they find enough to do just that."

All I could say to that was, "Shit."

"Shit's right, dude," Buster said. "I figure you're trying to find out what happened, so you better get to hopping." He looked over at Sonnenberg. "I'm assuming that if you got these two on your team you didn't do anything wrong, because they wouldn't be working for a guilty man. Good luck." He turned and left.

Sonnenberg sat on his sofa, his face pale, staring off at nothing in the middle distance.

Quincy walked over and put a hand on my shoulder.

"It's all on you now, Al," he said.

So, I thought, what else is new.

FOURTEEN

A number of things happen when a case I'm working on reaches a critical point; I have the strangest dreams, usually involving my late wife, Sara, who when alive was always a sounding board when I had a personal dilemma, and who gave great advice; I come up with some 'Hail Mary' plan that has about a fifty-fifty chance of failure; or I consult my friend Carlton Raine.

The problem with the dreams is that they're unpredictable. Before I met Sandra, I dreamed often of Sara and Nathan, and a time or two the dreams helped me figure out a particularly thorny issue, but lately I've not been having them as much. I think my subconscious is finally coming to accept my loss, or maybe it's just the passage of time.

I don't like operations that are put together on the fly; there are too many things that can go wrong. Only a few times have I felt that there was no other option, such as the time Buster and I took off to the West Virginia mountains without any kind of backup to rescue Sandra and his wife, Alma, from the clutches of a vicious militia leader who had kidnapped them in order to put pressure on Buster not to reveal an operation they feared he'd learned about. It worked, but it had been touch and go for a while, and I almost got my head blown off by a fragmentation grenade that, fortunately, blew the nuts off the militia leader instead.

Carlton 'Blood' Raine, a retired CIA agent who is in his eighties, but refuses to divulge his precise age, has been something of a mentor and father figure for me for a few years. One of the early black pioneers in the agency, he'd been a field agent specializing in direct action missions, a euphemism for clandestine combat operations, and had gotten the nickname, Blood,' not because it had been a common nickname for black men in the 1950s—not that any of his button-down, Ivy League colleagues at the time would be aware of that, or would dare use a racially-tinged nickname, even behind his back—but, because blood tended to flow in copious quantities in most of his operations.

Quincy introduced me to Blood during a particularly thorny case. A Chinese gangster that I'd helped put in prison had escaped and was getting his revenge on my by going after my friends and acquaintances. Though retired, Blood still had active contacts in the agency, and they often provided him with toys to test. He'd loaned me some of those toys to aid me in finding and capturing the gangster, and we became friends. That friendship was further cemented by the fact that I introduced him to Elizabeth Sung, a Chinese-American lawyer I'd met during the case, and who had also been targeted by the gangster. Despite the nearly fifty year difference in their ages, the chemistry between the two was instantaneous and solid, and it was not long after that Elizabeth moved from her Chinatown condo into Blood's cabin in the woods west of my place off River Road.

Blood's something of a fixture for me now. When I need to bounce ideas off someone who can see the tactical situation in the same way I do, and who can come up with operational ideas, I turn to him. When I just need someone to listen and let me circle around until I stumble across the answer to my own question, I turn to him.

After Buster left, I spent a few minutes reassuring Sonnenberg and Quincy that I wouldn't rest until I got to the bottom of the situation. Then I called Blood and told him I needed to talk.

He told me to come on out, but I detected a slight note of hesitancy in his voice, that I'd not heard before.

"Are you sure? I can come another time if

now is inconvenient," I said.

"Hey, young fella, you come on out," he said. "You know you're always welcome."

There was still something in his tone, but over the phone it's hard to get a good read on people. Something was amiss, but with nothing but his voice in my ear, I couldn't pin it down. Now, I had two reasons to see him.

I called Heather to let her know that I was going to see him, and that I'd probably go home afterwards instead of driving all the way back into town.

Getting from Sonnenberg's neighborhood to River Road in Montgomery County is tricky. It's tempting to get on Connecticut Avenue and drive north through Bethesda, but that way can get really backed up sometimes, especially as you get to the line between the District of Columbia and Maryland. While it's a longer drive, going south on Wisconsin Avenue, down past Georgetown University, to M Street, and then west to Canal Road, is actually shorter and less hectic. Traffic can get a little snarled at the south end of Wisconsin as it approaches M Street, when local residents, commercial trucks, and Georgetown students all come together, but once you get pass Hoya Stadium and get on Canal Road, you're in a different world. The Potomac River and the C&O Canal on one side, and a hill thickly covered with vegetation on the other, give you the impression you're in the countryside rather than on the edge of a big city.

An hour after leaving Sonnenberg's house, I was turning right off River Road onto the winding dirt track that makes its way through a stand of evergreens, oak, and walnut trees to the fortress-like log cabin Blood Raine calls home.

It's not exactly a place you'd stumble across by accident, unless you're the type who likes to drive down unmarked country lanes that are nothing more than tire tracks in the hard packed earth, with no signs to give you the faintest idea where you are. In fact, if you weren't paying attention as you drove down River Road, you'd miss the turnoff entirely. There's no sign, no mailbox, nothing to indicate that anyone lives at the end of the track.

While driving it I played my usual game of trying to spot the surveillance cameras I knew Blood had installed in the trees that grew fifty yards back on either side of the track, beyond the waist-high saw grass lining it. I did this partly out of curiosity, just to see if I could match a wily old spy, and partly because I figured if I could spot them, someone else could eventually as well, and I owed it to my friend to let him know. But, he was good. In several years of trying I had yet to get a glimmer of a camera lens or even a hint of a piece of equipment attached to a tree.

The reason I knew they were there,

though, was that he was always waiting for me on the front porch with a sly smile on his nut brown face. He'd probably been tracking my car from the moment I turned onto the track until I reached the last bend before the cabin came into sight. That gave him just enough time to get from the secured room behind his living room and out to the front porch.

He stood there, shoulders squared and back erect, with a bright glint in his brown eyes and a smile on his face. His hair, which he kept cropped short, was almost entirely white now, and as I got out of the car and approached the porch, I could see the glimmer of gray stubble on his square jaw. Underneath the plaid shirt he wore—I'd never seen him in short sleeves—he didn't look muscular, but when I grasped his hand I could feel the strength that was still in his muscles. Some people age gracefully. Carlton Raine was one of those people. His smile got broader when he released my hand.

"Hello, youngster," he said in that deep voice of his, with just a trace of a gentile southern accent. "It's been too long since you paid me a visit."

"I got the feeling on the phone that I might be interrupting something," I said.

His cheeks reddened and he looked away for a fraction of a second.

"Sometimes I forget how perceptive you can be," he said. "It's not really that much of an interruption. It's just that Liz and I were spending the day together. She decided to take a four-day weekend, and when you called, we were . . ."

As his speech drifted off, I noticed that the top button of his shirt was undone. Then, it was my turn to blush.

"Oh, I'm sorry, I should have known better."

"Should have known better than what? There's no way you could have figured out what I was doing over the phone. Anyway, it was time to come up for air, and I have missed talking to you, so come on in."

I hesitated. "Are you sure Elizabeth's okay with me barging in? I mean, I don't want to—"

He laughed. "Come on in. She's in the kitchen fixing some sandwiches for lunch. Heck, she'll be happy to see you, too. Too bad you didn't bring Sandra along."

As we walked into the living room, Elizabeth Sung came out of the kitchen. She was wearing short shorts and a yellow tee shirt, and the way they moved as she walked it was clear that she wasn't wearing anything else. Her bare feet made whispering sounds as she walked across the polished wood floor.

"Hello, Al," she said. "Welcome. Come on in, I have sandwiches and salad, and iced tea the way you like it." She walked over and pecked Blood on the cheek. "I thought it would be nice to eat on the porch, Carlton, darling. Why don't you and Al take three chairs out there while I get the food."

While she went back to the kitchen, Blood and I carried three folding camp chairs out and placed them on the porch in a position that enabled us to see the track clearly and have easy access to the door in case we had to go back inside quickly. Even though he'd been retired from the agency for decades, there were still people and organizations out there that remembered him and would love to catch him with his guard down. I could relate to his sense of caution. In restaurants and other places, I never sit with my back to the entrance, and usually try to place myself where I can see the entire space without having to crane my neck. You can never totally get away from your past, so you just have to learn to live with it the best you can.

Elizabeth came out just as we'd settled the chairs. She carried a silver tray with a pitcher of tea, three glasses, three small plates with thick club sandwiches on them, and three small bowls containing chopped spinach leaves, diced tomatoes and pine seeds. Blood took the tray and motioned her to the chair nearest the door. He sat in the center chair and handed her a sandwich and salad. He gave me one, and then poured three glasses of tea.

For a few minutes we ate in silence, enjoying the cool breeze blowing from the surrounding trees and the taste of the food.

When his sandwich was finished, Blood put the plate and the unfinished salad on the tray which he'd put on the floor near his feet. He took a sip of tea and sighed.

"Now, that hits the spot. You know, I never liked unsweetened tea until I met the two of you. Now, I don't know how I drank it sweet for so long."

"I'll never understand westerners," Elizabeth said. "You boil the tea, and then put ice in to make it cold. Then you put sugar in to make it sweet, which completely masks the taste of the tea."

"Come, come, my dear," Blood said, patting her hand. "You were born in this country, and I'll wager that Al and I have spent more time outside the U.S. than you have. You, my darling, are one of those westerners you're referring to."

She winked at him over the rim of her glass and laughed that musical laugh of hers. "Okay, so I like iced tea. Don't ever tell my mother that though. She'd disown me." She finished her drink and put her glass, plate and bowl on the tray. "Are you finished with your food Al? I'll take the empty dishes to the kitchen. I'll leave the tea here for you two."

Without waiting for my reply, she took the bowl and plate from my lap and put them next to the others on the tray. She put the pitcher on the porch, picked up the tray and went into the house, moving with a sinuous grace that I could not help but admire. Most men would be put off by another man looking at their woman like that, but Blood knew that I was only admiring the view and nothing else. I'm a one-woman man; not incapable of enjoying the view; but for me, looking was all I would do. Besides, before I'd introduced her to Blood, I'd had my chance with her and turned it down. She'd taken my rejection gracefully, especially after I'd explained my relationship with Sandra, and after she met Blood, I was consigned to the past as far as such things were concerned. She also understood my relationship with Blood, and kept that part of his life compartmented from what they had with each other, much like Sandra did with me—most of the time.

"She knows you want to discuss a case," Blood said. "So, she's giving us some privacy, just in case we say something that as a lawyer she'd be legally obliged to report to the authorities."

"Wow, you've trained her well."

"No, she came to that on her own. She has a general idea of what I did for the agency, and from her experience with you when that gangster kidnapped her, she knows how you operate. And, by the way, she personally approves, but she also takes her oath as an officer of the court seriously. I believe it's called plausible deniability."

Damn. A lawyer and a spy. What a combination. But, it works for me. I gave him a quick down and dirty summation of the case.

After I stopped talking, he just sat there silently for a moment. Then, he looked at me, his gaze piercing through me. "Let me ask you something, young fellow, and think hard before your answer; do you think this woman's still alive?"

I knew what he was doing. He was forcing me to reexamine my assumptions, to make sure I was going at the case in the right way rather than chasing down a blind alley, driven by my ego and need to be right. I took a deep breath.

"Yeah," I said. "I couldn't tell you why, but my gut tells me she's still alive."

"Just checking. For the record, I think you're probably right. Bodies aren't as easy to hide as people think. In addition, it wouldn't be easy to move a body, dead or alive, from a place like Brandywine Estates. Too much chance that someone might spot it."

I'd pretty much come to the same conclusion. "But, wouldn't hiding a body be just as difficult? I seriously doubt the whole staff of the inn and the vineyard's in on whatever is going on."

He rubbed the stubble on his cheek. "Right, so it would have to be some place out of the way with restricted or limited access to all but those who are part of the abduction."

I closed my eyes and visualized the layout at Brandywine, putting myself in the shoes of someone who wanted to keep a kidnap victim out of the public eye, someplace I had total control of.

"It couldn't be in the inn itself, too much danger of a member of the staff stumbling across it. So, it has to be one of the outbuildings."

"Good, good," he said. "Now, you're thinking. How many outbuildings?"

"Two, no, three. There's the machine shed. It's nearest the inn, but it's pretty open to view from the inn, so I'd rule it out. The only other possibilities would be the big building they call the cellar, and the one they keep the wine press in. Both are out of direct line of sight of the inn, and access as far as I could tell is restricted to the owner, Cuthbert, and two of his men."

"The problem will be getting some proof that they're holding her. So, how would you go about doing that?" He stared intently at me.

He did that sometimes; asking me questions, and forcing me to find my own conclusions, rather than just making suggestions. I respected him for that.

"Well, it's not likely they'd move during the day. Too many prying eyes. So, I'd need to have the place under surveillance when everyone else's asleep. The problem with that is it's not possible to watch both buildings at the same time in the dark, because I'd have to be in too close and I'd likely be spotted."

He smiled. "Now, I might just be able to

help you with that." He got up and went inside the house.

A few minutes later he returned carrying a plain, brown box about the size of a shoe box. After sitting down, he opened the box and tilted it so I could see the contents. I recognized them right away, night vision goggles, but they were a far cry from the clunky devices I'd seen soldiers use. He took them out and handed them to me. They didn't weigh much more than a ski cap. The head mount was a circular leather band with cross straps that fitted over the top of the head, a singular monocular viewer was attached to the head strap, and a leather chin strap looped down from it.

"I guess I shouldn't ask you where this came from, right."

"Best if you don't, and please don't lose or damage them, these things are expensive, and there are only a few prototypes. As you can see, it's for one eye only. Comes in handy if someone suddenly turns the lights on. You're left with one good eye. It has a short-range infrared illuminator so you can see things up close even in total darkness." He pointed to a protrusion on the side of the monocular. "And a long-range IR illuminator to increase the range, so you should be able to make out details from a couple hundred meters away."

"With this, I'll be able to see from far enough away to keep both buildings under surveillance. I don't know how to thank you, Blood."

He took the goggle from me and put it back in the box, then handed the box to me. He smiled and patted my hand.

"Just get that young woman home safe to her husband."

FIFTEEN

It was too late to do anything that day, so I took the goggles home and put them on the top shelf my closet where I keep my K-bar knife and other items I sometimes need on a case.

I debated telling Sandra what I was going to do, but then decided not to worry her. My plan was to go to Brandywine on Friday night after dark after everyone had gone to sleep. I would tell her, just before leaving for Brandywine, that I was doing a nighttime stakeout, nothing dangerous, but that it might take me all night. She wouldn't be happy about it, but if I called her from the office just before I took off, at least I wouldn't have to see the unhappiness on her face. I'd take my lumps, though, when I got back. Some people defer gratification. I defer pain.

The next morning, I called Buster from the house and asked him to meet me for breakfast, a break from our normal lunch routine, but I needed to run some things past him and my day would be busy. Buster has never been known to turn down a free meal, so he agreed.

I explained to Sandra, and after an early run, I changed and headed downtown to Mom's, our favorite place to eat and talk. She gave me a suspicious look, but said nothing. A little voice in the back of my mind whispered that she knew I was up to something, but was too much of a lady to call me on it. Made me feel a bit guilty for holding out on her, but I'd already gone past the point of no return. To bring it up on the way out to breakfast, I feared, would only upset her and ruin my breakfast, so I kissed her on the cheek, promised to make it up to her by taking her out for a special Sunday dinner, and beat a hasty retreat to my car. If that makes me sound cowardly, I plead guilty.

It took me almost an hour to get to Mom's on U Street near the revitalized Sixteenth Street corridor. That time of morning, finding a parking place within two blocks is all but impossible, but I found back street parking about four blocks away and hoofed it to the restaurant. Buster, who lives in the District, was already there, sitting in our customary table in the near right corner with a view of the room and the street.

Mom's is an institution, specializing in cooking and serving southern style soul food for nearly four decades, surviving the riots after Martin Luther King Jr.'s assassination in the 60s and gentrification that began transforming many of the mom and pop operations in the area in the late 1990s. In all that time, it's been presided over by the Queen Bee, Mom—no one seems to know her true name, and everyone's too afraid to ask—who was probably quite the bit of brown sugar forty years ago, but is now three hundred pounds of absolute ruler over her domain. When you enter Mom's, unless you're a first-time customer, you don't bother asking for a menu. Like the stereotypical Italian restaurant managers of the movies, she *tells* you what you're having, and then she sits by the cash register opposite the entrance and watches like an osprey waiting for a fish to get too near the surface of a lake to make sure you *eat* everything she served you. Buster and I eat lunch there three or four times a month, which is about all Alma will allow him, and which causes me to have to do a few extra miles the mornings after to shed the additional pounds Mom's cooking puts on—actually, not Mom herself, but her husband, who is even larger than she is, and is always in the kitchen. I heard Mom call him Calvin once, but in all the years I've been a customer have never spoken to him, or seen him speak to another customer. In fact, other than a smile or nod, he only communicates with his food.

Mom was at her usual place on the stool at the end of the counter near the cash register, wearing a tent of a dress—blue with large white polka dots—and a yellow apron big enough to make a two-man pup tent. Her cheeks quivered and jiggled as she saw me, and her dark brown face lit up in a smile.

"Hey, hon," she boomed. "You come up in here to try Mom's special breakfast I see. You must've done heard I doing blueberry pancakes?"

I hadn't, but I never argue with Mom. And, I wasn't about to remind her that it was Calvin doing the pancakes. I nodded and smiled. "With all the trimmings, okay," I said.

She oozed off the stool. "You gone and set yourself down with that no-good friend of yours, I'll bring you some coffee. Food be ready directly."

She has a long list of names for my no-good friend, Buster Mayweather, and none of them are good. A stranger would think she didn't like him the way she talked about him. But, the truth was, Mom looked at both of us like the sons I suppose she never had. Me, she viewed as the dutiful son who would always do the right thing, and didn't need any discipline, while Buster was the son who is always up to mischief, and in need of a good talking to, but who she loved just as much. That was clear the way she never passed him without laying her huge hand gently on his shoulder, or rubbing the side of his face. And, the big galoot loved every coddling minute of it.

He put his mug down as I approached the table.

"Hey, Buster," I said. "Thanks for meeting me so early in the morning."

"Hey, gotta eat breakfast anyway, bro, and Mom's is as good a place as any to do that. Alma's into one of them health food kicks again, making me eat oat bran and some other rabbit food three meals a day now."

"It'll help you live longer, you know."

"What's the point of living a long time if you miserable," he said.

I sat down with my back partially to the wall, and like magic Mom appeared at my elbow with a mug of coffee.

"I got to say," she said. "He right 'bout that. Man got to have protein in his diet or his muscle go all limp and useless." Then she looked down at me with an impish smile. "And, I mean *every* muscle go limp and useless, if you know what I mean."

I did know what she meant. My cheeks burned. Mom takes advantage of her age and usually says whatever comes to her mind. I'm a bit on the old-fashioned side, and she was something of a surrogate mother, so hearing her throw out suggestive language like that was unsettling. Buster, on the other hand, appeared to either not notice, or more likely, not care.

"See, even Mom agrees with me that eating nothing but rabbit food ain't good for you."

"Now, you boys drink your coffee while I go kick my no-good husband's butt to get your food out here." Now, that I'd pay to see. Calvin had to have a hundred pounds on her, and the looks of a man who could hold his own in a rough and tumble, and Mom's legs were so huge, I couldn't see her lifting them high enough to reach his butt.

She turned and walked off. The verb walk, though, is hardly adequate to describe what Mom's large body does when she walks, or what it looks like from the rear. Let's just say, two large weather balloons bobbing up and down in the wind, and let it go at that.

"Now, bro," Buster said. "I like your company and all, and I love Mom's down home breakfasts, but I know you didn't ask me to have breakfast with you 'cause of my good looks. What's up?"

I had to choose my next words carefully. Like Elizabeth, he was obligated by his position to report any illegal activity, even if a friend was involved, and what I was planning pretty much amounted to breaking and entering, or at a minimum trespassing.

"Look, amigo, I think the Fauquier authorities are looking in the wrong direction on this Leana Sonnenberg case."

"You mean them thinking the husband did her in?"

"That," I said. "And that she's been killed in the first place." At his puzzled look, I explained my reasoning.

"That makes sense, makes a lot of sense, except for one thing; how you gonna establish a link between her and this Cuthbert dude?"

"I'm working on that . . . well, actually, Heather's working on it. One other avenue I plan to follow is talk to her sister again. I'm hoping she might have told her something about her time in the army that'll help me make a connection."

"Okay, that makes sense, but what do you want from me?"

"I need to do a little more snooping around Brandywine Estates, and I need you to let your friends in Fauquier County know I'm not stepping on their toes."

His eyes narrowed to tiny slits, but he smiled. I was busted, but since I hadn't said explicitly that I planned anything illegal, he was under no obligation to report me.

"First off, bro, county cops ain't usually on my Christmas card list, and county sheriffs are lower on the list than county police because they're more political. I will, though, call and ask them to extend professional courtesy. Could I give you a piece of advice . . . as a friend?"

"You know you can," I said.

"Try not to get caught."

Charles Ray

SIXTEEN

After a breakfast that forced me to let my belt
out a notch, I called Laura Colman's number
and made arrangements to stop by her
house, and then called Heather to let her
know I'd be even later getting to the office.
Like Sandra, she's accustomed to my way of
doing things, and didn't waste time
questioning me as to why.

I was driving mainly against traffic from
Mom's across town to Foggy Bottom, and got
lucky and found a two-hour empty parking
space a block past Laura's house.

She met me at her door, barefoot and
wearing Bermuda shorts and a scoop neck
blouse. Her hair was mussed and her face
was puffy around eyes that looked like she'd
been on a two-day bender. She had a hang
dog look on her face, and didn't look

particularly happy to see me, but she stepped to the side and inclined her head for me to enter.

"Sorry to barge in on you like this," I said. "I hope I'm not interrupting your work."

"Not at all. I haven't been able to get much work done anyway. Would you like a cup of tea or coffee? Any word on Leana?" The words tumbled out of her mouth, but her eyes weren't really focused on the here and now. It was like listening to a tape recorder, and made me wonder if she might be on something.

"A cup of coffee would be fine, and I don't have anything new on your sister, but I am here to talk about her."

She turned away and walked toward the kitchen in the back of the house, her shoulders slumped. I noticed that she was barefoot, and that the bottoms of her feet were smudged as if she'd neglected to wipe her feet after walking outside. In addition, there was a tear in the hem of the gray sweatshirt she wore.

"Talk, talk," she mumbled. "That's all anyone ever wants to do. When is someone going to *do* something?"

I didn't think she really expected me to answer, which was just as well, since I didn't really have an answer to give her.

She already had a pot of coffee brewed. She filled two ceramic mugs, taking the one with a chip out of the rim and handing me the other. She hooked her toes on the lower rim of a stool and pulled it next to the one her hips were perched on. I pulled it closer and settled myself on it. After blowing on the coffee, I took a sip. It was instant. Why anyone would buy a coffee maker, and then use it to heat water to pour over instant coffee, is beyond me, and to add insult to injury it tasted like some off-brand, leaving a metallic aftertaste on my tongue. I put the mug on the counter.

"Look, I know you're upset, anyone would be under the circumstances, but I have a good feeling that your sister, though perhaps in some danger, is otherwise okay."

She put her mug down and dug her knuckles into her eyes, then looked at me, her mouth in a little 'o.' "She's in danger, but she's all right? What the hell does that even mean?"

"Don't worry about it now," I said. "I need to ask you some questions about your sister's time in the army, especially the last few years before she got out."

"What does her time in the army have to do with anything?"

Her tone was belligerent, and I was in danger of losing control of the situation. "Let's just say that I think someone from that period in her life is involved. Look, I don't have time to explain it now, but trust me; I think I'm onto something." I put as much confidence into my voice as I could manage, and looked her directly in the eyes.

In general, most people want to be told that things are under control, and that the world will unfold according to plan. Con men use that fact of human nature to gull people into falling for their scams. But, con men are psychopathic, narcissistic manipulators who do it because they can, and because they get a rush out of screwing over other people. All of us, though, have a bit of the con artist in us. We use tone of voice, body posture, and soothing words to manipulate the people around us on a daily basis. It's the oil that sometimes keeps the wheels of relationships in motion. 'Fake it until you make it,' is the mantra of a lot of successful business people. I wasn't completely 'faking it.' I did think Leana was still alive. I just didn't yet have a clue as to what I was going to do about it. At any rate, my tone of voice, or my body language worked. Laura relaxed, and her expression was no longer so combative.

"Okay," she said. "But, Leana didn't really like talking too much about that time in her life."

"Yeah, but I figure she'd occasionally share things with you. I'm mainly interested in the time she spent at Fort Belvoir; those last few months or weeks before she decided to leave the army."

She screwed up her eyes in concentration. "That's the time I think that bummed her out the most," she said. "You know, she'd been thinking about staying in the army, to 'get her twenty' is how she used to put it. They were even arranging for her to train to become an officer. I mean, she was really excited there for a while." A shadow of sadness and anger fell over her face. "Then, overnight, things changed. She clammed up for a while and wouldn't talk about it, but I could tell that something was terribly wrong."

I just continued to look at her with an expression of interest on my face. The art of getting information out of people is less about asking questions—although, asking the *right* questions is important—it's about listening. And, by listening, I mean *active* listening. Using your body language and facial expressions to let people know that what they're saying at the moment is the most important thing in the world to you. This will often get them to answer your question before you even ask it.

"But," she continued. "I finally got some of it out of her. It turns out that not everyone in her outfit was as supportive as she thought. One of the colonels was out to get her. Started all kinds of vicious rumors about misbehavior—all lies by the way—until the pressure got so bad, Leana just said 'fuck it' and turned in her walking papers."

"Did she ever go into detail about the rumors?"

"Yeah, some. This ass hole was spreading shit like, Leana was sleeping with some of her male passengers, or she was helping them procure whores, crap like that. I mean, she could've been thrown in jail for doing shit like that, and it for sure wouldn't help her become an officer."

"Did she ever tell you why someone would do a thing like that to her?"

She nodded slowly. "Sure. It had something to do with this colonel holding secret meetings with some guy, and envelopes being passed, but she'd never tell me exactly what that meant."

"She ever tell you the colonel's name?"

"Uh-uh, just said he was one of the big shots in test and development or something." She picked her mug up and held it against her breasts. As she looked at me, her eyes glistening, I saw the lost little girl who had come to depend on her big sister, now scared of maybe having to face the world without her.

"Don't worry, Laura," I said. "I'm gonna get your sister back."

She just sat there, clasping that mug and not really looking at me, or hearing me. There was nothing else I could say or do, so I just squeezed her shoulder and stood there for a moment. Finally, she looked up at me.

"Please," she said in a voice barely above a whisper. "She's all I have left."

SEVENTEEN

It was nearing lunch when I left Laura Colman's place, so I swung across the Roosevelt Bridge onto Arlington Boulevard, got off at the Rosslyn exit and entered Fort Myer through the back gate near the Iwo Jima Memorial and Netherlands Carillion sites. I drove past the big houses where some of the army's top generals live, past the chapel adjacent to Arlington National Cemetery, and over toward the Washington Boulevard gate to the Post Exchange, where I had a hot dog and coke at the PX food court. After that, I exited onto Washington Boulevard, swung behind the Pentagon and onto I-395 back across the Potomac into the District.

After parking in one of the three slots reserved for us by the building management,

I went upstairs to the office.

"Did you learn anything useful from Laura Colman?" Heather asked as I entered.

"She couldn't give a name, but Leana did tell her that she'd had a run-in with some colonel at Fort Belvoir. That's why she left the army." I gave her the details I'd gotten from Laura.

"I think we can assume the colonel in question is one Harlan Cuthbert," she said. "Of course, we still don't have concrete proof."

"I'm hoping to get that tonight."

She opened her mouth, snapped it shut, and then looked at me with a naked look of skepticism.

"You're going back to Brandywine," she said.

"Yeah."

"And, you don't plan to announce your arrival."

"Or my presence unless it becomes necessary," I said.

She just sat there looking at me for ten seconds. "Don't you think it'd be a good idea to take along some backup?"

"You mean you?"

"Why not? I might be small, but I have a black belt in karate."

She does, and while she's not as strong as me, or as athletic as Sandra, I have no doubt that she can handle herself in most situations. This mission, though, had to be solo. I had a hunch that Cuthbert's two henchmen could be at the limits of my ability, and totally beyond hers. There was no way I was putting her at risk. I wouldn't tell her that, though. She'd take my head off if I did.

"This is just a recon," I said. "I have a hunch Cuthbert's holding Leana hostage in one of the outbuildings. I want to confirm that."

"And, if she is there?"

That was part of the plan that was still a little fuzzy. Actually, until that moment I hadn't really thought about what I'd do if I discovered that she was there.

"In that case, I guess I'll have to try and rescue her."

"And, that, boss man, is where you'll probably need backup."

She was nothing if not persistent. I had to put a final stake in it, though.

"Look, Heather," I said. "I know you're fully licensed now, and I've no doubt you can take care of yourself in most situations, but this is a night op in completely unfamiliar terrain. While I know it a little, you've never been there before, so you'd be handicapped, and, no insult intended, you'd slow me down."

Her eyes narrowed to slits. Her lips turned down.

"I'll grant you, that's probably right, but shouldn't you at least ask Buster to go along?"

"No, I can't put him in a position like that. It's out of his jurisdiction, and technically I'll be trespassing. If Leana's there, I doubt the Fauquier County authorities will pursue a trespassing charge, but it wouldn't look good for him either way, so this one has to be solo."

I could see from the steely expression on her face that she wasn't about to give up so easy. Hell, in her place, I would probably have done the same. I'd never let my partner go out without doing all that I could to help, and she'd learned well from me on that score. Finally, her expression brightened.

"I have an idea that just might take care of your back up," she said. "Provided, that is, that you'll agree."

"I'm listening."

It was so damn simple I mentally kicked myself for not thinking of it.

"Give me the number for the sheriff's office. If you spot Leana, call me, and I'll call them. That way, you can keep your attention focused on Leana, knowing that backup's on the way."

"You want to call and tell them I'm illegally snooping around?"

"No, silly, I'll tell them that we got an anonymous tip . . . maybe someone you met on the inn staff when you visited before . . . and they called and reported seeing something suspicious. You went out to check on it so we wouldn't be wasting their time on a wild goose chase, and . . . oh, don't worry, I'll think of a story when I get them on the phone."

A bit on the complicated side, but I had no doubt she'd be able to pull it off. She'd come up with a modification to my operation, and snookered me into accepting her as my backup, albeit from a distance, but backup's backup, wherever it's stationed, and I was impressed with the way she thought on her feet.

"Sounds like a plan." I gave her Mansfield's name card. "This is one of the detectives handling the case, and this is his direct number."

"Will he respond?"

"Oh, if you tell him that I'm back at Brandywine, he'll respond all right." Hell, he'd probably break every speed limit in the book thinking he was going to get the chance to bust me. "Now, I'm going into my office and relax for a couple of hours before I hit the road."

Charles Ray

EIGHTEEN

I got on the road at 4:00 to beat the Friday afternoon rush hour, but US-29 was still pretty crowded until well past Fairfax City. The stretch through Manassas wasn't too crowded, and as I neared the Warrenton turnoff and the road to Brandywine, most of the traffic was coming toward me, so I was able to drive my usual ten miles per hour over the speed limit of 45.

I stopped at a Seven-Eleven and bought two quart-sized mugs of iced coffee—no sense buying hot coffee that would be cold by the time I got around to drinking it, and I just needed the caffeine to help me stay awake—four Snickers chocolate bars and two one-liter bottles of water. I could have brought my thermos from home, but I figured if Sandra saw me hauling it out of the pantry, it might cause her to question me about my plans. I'd kind of hinted that this could just be a short recon mission. She's pretty good about what I do, but a few close calls have made her worry every time I put on my black recon outfit—which I wasn't wearing this time for that very reason. I wanted her to think this was just a normal stakeout. That was my preferred attire, but my blue jeans and dark blue long sleeved shirt would have to do. At least I had the fact that Cuthbert and his crew wouldn't be expecting me.

I arrived at the turnoff at 5:50. It was still light out, would still be light until around 7:00 or 8:00, so I pulled off the road and sat there a while planning the next step. My throat was a bit dry, so I took a few sips of water to soothe it. I resisted the coffee, as much as I wanted a taste. Caffeine activates the bladder as quickly as beer, and there was no place along the road to take a leak without risking being seen by a passing car. All I needed was to have some concerned Virginia citizen calling the local authorities to report a black man pissing along the side of the road.

That also meant I couldn't park in one place too long. I needed to find a place to stash my car while I made my way on foot to a point from which I could put the cellar and wine press buildings under surveillance. Then, I remembered the park just outside Brandywine's fence. Even though it was probably closed at night, and parking wasn't allowed, I didn't think the police patrolled this area frequently enough that it would present a problem. I started the engine, pulled back onto the road and drove slowly until I saw the park on the left, and Brandywine's arched sign ahead came into view. I turned into the park and drove to the farthest end of the tar and gravel parking lot, stopping under an expansive oak tree, hoping the dark shadows of the tree would ensure that my green Volkswagen wouldn't be noticeable from the road.

After waiting a few minutes to make sure I hadn't raised any alarms, I grabbed a couple of Snickers bars and put them in my pocket. I then took the night vision goggles from the box and draped them over my arm, and with a container of coffee in one hand, and water in the other, I made my way through the bushes at the end of the park to the fence that surrounded Brandywine. I pushed the coffee and water containers through the gaps in the fence and sat them down on the gritty earth. Then, I slipped the night vision goggles onto my head, pushing the monocular aside since there was still enough ambient light allowing me to make my way along the wide space between rows of grape vines without the extra assistance.

I climbed over the fence, retrieved my water and coffee, and stood still for thirty seconds, listening to see if my presence had caused any disruption in the normal night sounds. All I heard was the soft whisper of a gentle breeze brushing across the leaves, the croaking of frogs from the park behind me, and the 'coo, coo' sound of mourning doves from somewhere off to my left front. The only human presence I sensed was my own.

I guessed the inn to be almost directly in front of me if I stood with my back to the fence. That meant my targets were some twenty to twenty-five degrees to my left. Absolute accuracy wasn't necessary. All I needed to do was get near the end of the rows of vines, find a place from which I could see both buildings, and stay down out of sight. Oh, and move through a tangle of vines and the scaffolding upon which they hung without making any noise. Piece of cake.

I took my time walking, making sure to stay in the center of the clear space between the rows of vines. Brushing against the trellised vines wouldn't make a loud noise, but I was guessing that Cuthbert's men were trained soldiers, and to a soldier, the sound of a body brushing against foliage, at night, from an area where a body is not supposed to be, is as loud as a fire alarm going off right next to your ear.

From the beginning of the fence to the clear space around the outbuildings was a quarter mile. That's 1,320 feet. The length of my normal step is three feet. That's 440 steps, actually a few less, to my objective. Doesn't sound like much, does it? When you're walking in the dark, in unfamiliar territory, trying not to be spotted, it seems to take forever. You walk ten to fifteen steps, taking your time so you don't stumble into something, step in a groundhog's hole, trip over a downed tree limb, or stub your toe on a rock. Then, you stop, and make a complete 360, looking, smelling, and listening for any change that might signal a threat. Even when you're not burdened with a weapon, a full load of ammo, and a forty-pound ruck, it's tiring, and a tiny bit nerve wracking. Every sound is magnified. The buzz of a dragonfly is a bullet whizzing through the air. The whistle of a night bird is a signal from a hidden ambusher.

At about half the distance to the edge of the field, the direction of the rows changed, from north-south to east-west. I had to slowly work my way through the rows by getting down and basically crawling beneath the vines. Fortunately, the heavy foliage started a foot above the ground, so I didn't brush against anything.

By the time the light area ten yards in front of me signaled that I was nearing the end of the field, and despite the chill in the air, my body was clammy with sweat under the long-sleeve cotton pullover I wore, and I had to focus hard to keep my heart rate down.

I crouched down a few feet back from destination, hunkering under an overhang of vines. I'd done a good job of dead reckoning navigation. The machine shed was slightly off to my right and the large cellar building to my left. In the gap between the two, the wine press building was a dark, block against the purple-black of the night sky. Lights at the corners of the machine shed illuminated the foreground sufficiently that I'd be able to see anyone approaching the cellar without the goggles, but the rearmost building was wrapped in dark shadows. Blood had known what he was doing, giving me the monocular device. With it, I'd be able to watch the near buildings with my naked eye, while scoping out the back building with the NVG.

A quick scan from right to left revealed that there was no one moving about outside, although I could see flickering shadows in the large front windows of the inn. I took a quick glance at my watch. The luminous green dial showed 9:02. By 10:00 it would be completely dark, and I figured that the inn's guests would all be tucked in by midnight, leaving me with little to do for nearly three hours. I smoothed the ground at the base of the vines, nestled down with my back supported by the trellis, and began what has to be the most boring, unattractive task of a private investigator, next to doing document searches—waiting for something to happen.

Except for the gentle whisper of the breeze, the sometimes raucous call of night birds and insects, and the muffled hum of the air conditioning units at the cellar and the wine press building, it was quiet, and for the first few hours of my vigil nothing happened.

That, unfortunately, is how it usually is, whether you're on a stakeout or a military patrol. Long periods of nothing. The real danger in situations like this is that the boredom can cause your attention to lapse. It only takes a few seconds of inattention to miss something important. The way I'd learned on long, boring military patrols to avoid this was to find some mental activity that allowed me to keep part of my mind focused on something that would keep me awake while leaving enough to stay laser-focused on my target. Some routine, repetitive action works, like naming the U.S. presidents in order, or matching presidents with the states they came from. The game I chose sitting there in the vineyard not only kept me awake, but, because it was related to what I was doing, helped keep most of my attention on my target.

The monocular took some getting accustomed to. Peering through it with one eye, seeing everything in shades of black and green with fuzz around the edges caused by the spillover of light from the shaded bulbs at the corner of the machine shed, caused a mild headache if I did it for longer than five minutes. So, to mitigate the headache, give me a chance to check out the areas bathed in the dim light, and stay awake, I set a limit of four minutes through the monocular with my left eye, followed by five minutes with both eyes scanning the area from the inn to the Cellar. Since I couldn't be constantly glancing down at my watch, I had to count off the minutes in my head. It was boring, but it kept me awake. To relieve some of the boredom, every twenty minutes, I'd flip the monocular up, and take a sip of coffee or water while I scanned the area with my naked eyes.

After a couple of hours of this, it became just too boring, so I added a little exercise where I listened for the sounds of nature and tried identifying them, still keeping the rotation of eyes to avoid the headaches.

The rustling sound behind me might have spooked anyone else, thinking it might be a snake, but I knew better. It was something like a squirrel or rabbit moving through the foliage. Had it been a snake, I never would have heard it. I thin heard a fluttering sound. Something with relatively large wings was flying near. The fluttering suddenly stopped; there was a cutoff 'shriek,' and then more fluttering. An owl or a hawk, probably an owl, since hawks do most of their hunting during daylight hours, had spotted some small creature and swooped down for a midnight snack.

Nature's pretty harsh like that. Big things feed on small things, and are in turn eaten by bigger things.

You've probably figured it out now. I was

bored. That's actually the biggest danger in an operation like this; getting bored and letting your mind wander. In combat it can get you killed. In my case it would mean I might miss something important. I gave myself a mental slap to refocus my mind.

I turned my attention back to the task at hand. Just in time to see a dark figure slip off the side of the inn's verandah, pass through a pool of dark shadow and emerge into the dim light at the farthest end of the employee parking lot. It was difficult to see details with my naked eye, but fortunately, the figure moved into the shadow of a large tree, enabling me to use the NVG. Even as a green and black figure, Lindsey was recognizable. He was carrying a large Styrofoam ice chest with a handle, and when he moved out of sight behind the machine shop, I guessed he'd be heading for the wine press building.

My guess turned out to be right. A few seconds later, he appeared at the left rear of the machine shop, angled toward the wine press building.

At the small door, he put the chest down and reached toward the keypad. Even with the goggles, I couldn't see what numbers he pressed on the six-button pad, but I could see the movement of his arm and shoulder. *Punch*-pause-*punch, punch*-pause-*punch.* He pulled the door open. Lindsey picked up the chest, went inside and closed the door. I snapped my eye shut just as the light inside the building came on.

I took my phone out and dialed. Heather answered on the first ring.

"Al, have you found her?" No messing around for this woman.

"Yeah," I said. "At least, I think so. I believe they're holding her in the building they keep the wine press in."

"Do I need to give any kind of directions?"

"No, just tell Mansfield I'll be in the wine press building. He'll know where it is . . . and, Heather, tell him to hurry.

"You got it, boss." She broke the connection.

My watch read 1:04. Warrenton was not too far away, and there wouldn't be that much traffic that time of morning. I figured twenty, thirty minutes tops, and the place would be crawling with cops. Cuthbert and his henchmen would have no place to go. I just had to make sure they stayed in place that long. Oh, and did I mention, stay alive in the process. Yeah, it was that kind of plan.

I looked around to make sure no one else was coming, and seeing no one, flipped the monocular up and slipped out of the foliage. I raced through the parking lot, past the machine shed, and across the gravel to the door of the building Lindsey had entered. I waited and listened, but heard no sounds on the other side of the door.

Turning my attention to the door, I flipped the monocular down to see the pad more clearly. The buttons, six in an unnumbered vertical row set in a rectangular metal pad with a black—as seen through the NVG—surface. I pulled up a mental image of Lindsey's movements when he keyed it. He'd raised his hand, so the first number was near the top. Figuring they wouldn't use the topmost button, my guess was that the first number was '2.' He'd then paused a fraction of a second and lowered his hand before pressing again—two quick punches, and then another pause, he'd lowered his hand, and pressed. Again, I assumed the bottommost number wouldn't be used, making the last number '5.' That left only the middle two, '3' and '4.' If I got the order wrong, I could always try again, but it would be better to get it on the first try. I tried to put myself in Cuthbert's mind. He would need a combination that wouldn't be obvious to anyone stumbling on it, but easy enough for his two minions to remember. The military mind tends to opt for the most logical move, and the GIs I'd worked with in the army always took the easy way, so it figured they'd select '3-4' in that order. Taking a deep breath, I punched '2-5-3-4' and grasped the door knob.

I turned it slowly, and to my relief, it rotated easily and silently. I pulled the door open a fraction of an inch and put my bare eye to the slit. It was still lit up inside, but I heard no movement.

I pulled the door open, just enough to allow me to squeeze through the crack. Once inside, I slowly pulled it shut, and stood there with my back against it, surveying the room.

Except for me, the machinery, and the stacks of barrels, the place was empty. That's what my eyes and ears told me, but my mind was having trouble with the concept. I'd just seen Lindsey enter this building, and there was only one door. He *had* to be there.

Most people, when outdoors, seldom look up. Indoors, believe it or not, people generally don't look down—or, at least, they don't notice things much below waist level. Years of combat patrols in environments where inattention could get you killed had taught me to look *everywhere*. So, standing at the door, I began a thorough scan of the room, starting overhead, downward, ending with a side-to-side scan of the floor. That's when I noticed three things that I'd paid no attention to when I first visited.

The conduit from the air conditioner unit attached to the outside wall entered and ran up the wall branched off in three directions, to the left and right toward outlet vents spaced evenly around the top of the wall, and downward, disappearing through the floor. There were faint traces of foot prints in the dust on the floor, leading up to the wine barrels stacked on the wooden pallet. One of the prints was cut off right at the edge of the pallet. On the wall just behind the stack of barrels was a gray metal plate with a circular red button. There was no label to identify its function, but the conduit running from the bottom of the plate went down, and like the air conditioner conduit, disappeared into the floor.

It only took my brain a few seconds to connect all the dots. The reason I didn't see Lindsey was that he'd gone down into a room or chamber underneath the building. How did he get there, you might ask? Why, the pallet of barrels sat over the hatch or doorway to the underground room, which was cooled by the air conditioning conduit, and the pallet was moved or the hatch opened, or both, by pressing the red button.

After coming to that conclusion, I still hesitated. In the dark I hadn't been able to see if Lindsey was armed, but I assumed that he was. I didn't know what lay below; would I open it up only to find a gun stuck in my face? What did he have in that chest he carried?

Standing around with my thumb up my ass, though, wasn't really an option. When I have a choice between doing nothing or doing something, my inclination is to try *something* and hope I'll be able to adjust course if I run into difficulty. Not, mind you, that I'm the rash, jump into a dark room type. But, jumping *from* a dark room's an entirely different matter. I reached for the light switch near the door, flipped it off, and put the monocular over my eye.

The foot prints in the dust stood out even more through the NVG goggle, and I could see little streaks where the pallet had slid along the floor. I walked over to the button, black rather than red through the goggle, and stood as close to the wall as possible before giving it a little push.

I'd expected a lot of noise, but the pallet silently lifted an inch and began sliding smoothly away from me. The rear end made a slight 'skiss' sound against the floor as it moved. After only a few inches, a black cavity began to reveal itself, and I could see a steep wooden staircase leading downwards. Leaning over, I peered down. The steps went down about ten feet, ending in a small rectangular space in front of a wooden door. The shades of black and green gave the scene the appearance of a poorly made horror movie, and in those movies there's always something pretty gruesome waiting behind the door at the bottom of the stairs.

Slowly, ever so slowly, I made my way down the stairs, trying not to cough from the dust hanging in the air of the narrow staircase. At the bottom, I lifted the monocular away and put my ear to the door. I could hear muffled voices through the wood, but couldn't make out any of the words.

Now was crunch time. My guess was that there were two people beyond the door; Lindsey and Leana Sonnenberg, and I hoped my guess was right. I was screwed if not. The way the door was set in the frame, it opened inward, indicating that the space beyond was probably large, and the volume of sound through the wood of the door indicated that the speakers were several feet away from it. The entrance door to the building had opened soundlessly, and I was hoping the same care had been taken with this door. I didn't need squeaky hinges alerting Lindsey of my presence too soon.

Assuming he wouldn't be working in the dark, I swiveled the monocular up and waited a few seconds to let my eyes adjust to the dark. Then, with my fingertips, I started gingerly pushing the door.

I was in luck. It swung inward without making a sound, and I stepped through. I'd guessed right. The space beyond the door was lit up by several 100-watt bulbs hanging from large wooden beams that supported the floor of the building above.

The space was like the set of an old horror movie. The floor was hard packed clay, and the walls, carved from the rock and subsoil, were lined with dark wooden beams. Crates of various sizes lined the walls to my left and right, stacked six feet high and stretching back for over twenty feet. While I was curious about the crates, it was the scene near the back of the space that really drew my eye.

Rob Lindsey, the chest he'd been carrying at his feet, stood over a figure tied to a wooden chair. I didn't need a program to know that it was Leana. Her arms were tied to the arms of the chair with cords, and her ankles were bound to the legs. Her hair was a mess, and she had a beauty of a shiner around her left eye. The right side of her face was a ruddy color, probably from being slapped. As Lindsey loomed over her, though, with his fists bunched tightly at his side, she glared up at him with defiance in her eyes.

"You can hit me all you want," she said with a voice that, though, cracked and weary, still projected strength. "I'm not telling you a damn thing."

"That's what you think, bitch," Lindsey growled. "You're gonna talk. In the end, everybody talks."

"Give it your best shot, you bastard."

I had to give her one thing; she was one tough cookie. I could see why she'd chosen truck driving as her army specialty. Unfortunately, Lindsey was no feather weight when it came to toughness. He pulled a folded knife from his pocket. When he pushed the button at the end of the handle, it made a 'snick!' sound and a wicked looking, six-inch blade snapped out.

"I plan to do just that," he said. "I'm gonna start by cuttin' off the end of your fuckin' nose. Then, I'm gonna kinda slice up that face of yours, so ain't nobody gonna wanta look at you ever again. If that don't work, maybe I'll cut your tits off. How'd you like that, bitch?"

I'd moved to the side so his body blocked me from her sight, but I could see her right side, and saw the jerking of her hand. He'd finally found the right button to push. Hell, that'd get to me, so I couldn't blame her. She'd held out for a long time, forcing them to resort to such crude threats. I moved forward, lifting my feet and putting them down toes first on the hard earth to avoid noise, stopping about six feet from Lindsey's back.

"Actually, I don't think so," I said. "In fact, I think you should just drop the knife and give yourself up."

He whirled, the knife held at his waist, looking surprised at first, but quickly taking on a look of anger.

"You're that private dick that was snoopin' around the other day. What the fuck you doin' here?"

"I'm here to take Ms. Sonnenberg home," I said.

"I don't think so, dude. In fact, you ain't never goin' home again."

He wasn't a bluffer, one of those guys who talks about what they're about to do to you. But, he was also no expert knife fighter. He lunged forward, thrusting the knife ahead of him, his arm outstretched.

It was a simple matter to pivot to the right, allowing the knife to slide bare millimeters past my chest. But, it was enough. It had him off balance, and his knife hand at my mercy. I grabbed the wrist with my right hand and pulled his forearm against my chest, pushing forward and turning to the right at the same time. This pulled him forward and caused him to lean forward, exposing the right side of his back. I jabbed him in the kidney with my left fist. He made an 'oomph' sound and bent at the knees. Without giving him a chance to recover, I raised his right arm and brought it down hard against the top of my raised right thigh. There was a loud 'snap' followed by a shrill screech as the pain from his broken forearm raced from the nerve receptors in his arm to his brain. I punched the right side of his head, just above and in front of the temple, and the screeching stopped like a radio being suddenly switched off and he slumped forward face down on the dirt floor.

Leana Sonnenberg looked up at me with gratitude on her dirt-streaked face. "I don't know who you are mister, but thanks," she said. "Now, could you untie me so we can get the hell out of here?"

I pulled the goggle off and put it on top of a crate of M72 LAW light anti-tank weapons. I then knelt down and took out my K-Bar.

"Not so fast, Mr. Pennyback." Cuthbert's voice came from behind me. "I'm afraid neither of you are going anywhere just yet."

NINETEEN

I slipped the K-Bar under my shirt, and tucked it into my belt. I looked up at Leana and winked. Her acknowledging nod was barely perceptible, but there was no mistaking the smile on her battered face. I stood slowly, and turned even more slowly. The last thing you want to do in a situation where someone has the drop on you is make a sudden move that might cause a finger to tighten on a trigger. When I turned and got a good look at what was behind me, I realized that it had been the wise thing to do.

Cuthbert stood there just inside the doorway with the business end of an M9 9mm automatic pointed at my midsection. Behind him, silhouetted by the light from the room above, stood Ken Bell with an M4 .556

carbine cradled across his chest. Both of them had expressions on their faces that spelled nothing but trouble for me. I raised my hands to my shoulders, and tried to look as non-threatening as possible; not difficult considering that they held all the cards at the moment. That's a euphemistic way of saying that they had the drop on me. The only weapon I had was my K-Bar knife which was strapped to my right ankle.

"I knew you were trouble the first time I laid eyes on you," Cuthbert said. "But, I must say, you surprised me. I didn't think you'd tumble on our little . . . secret."

As I looked around, I realized that Leana's location wasn't the secret he was referring to. Now, though, I had time to take a better look at all the crates stacked along the walls. The stenciling on the wooden sides was faded, but I could make out enough to know that I'd stumbled into something bigger than a simple kidnapping.

The box nearest to me had 'U.S. Army, M3 MAAWS' stenciled in faded black lettering. I recognized the Multi-role, Anti-tank, Anti-armor Weapons System. It was being introduced into the army's inventory around the time I retired. One of those babies could punch through a tank's side like a hot knife through a block of butter, and when they exploded inside the vehicle's hatch, no one inside survived. Next to that was a crate of M67 fragmentation grenades. It went on and on for as far as I could make out down both sides. He had enough armaments in this hold in the ground to equip a small army.

"Well, well, it looks like you have quite the little arms smuggling operation here," I said. Sometimes I can't resist being a bit lippy.

Cuthbert wasn't amused. "Yes, and I'm not about to let a dick like you mess it up." He spoke over his shoulder to Bell. "Ken, go up and keep a watch on the door. Let me know if anyone comes this way."

"Shouldn't I stay and help you get rid of this piece of shit, boss?" He looked down at Lindsey who still hadn't moved. I guess I hit him harder than I thought.

Cuthbert laughed gruffly.

"I know how much you'd like to get revenge for what he did to Rob, but I can handle it." He waved the M9 for emphasis. "I'll let you do the broad as soon as she spills her guts, how's that?"

Bell grinned wolfishly.

"Yeah, that'll do. Make the fucker suffer before you do 'im, okay?"

"It'll be my pleasure."

Bell smiled broadly, saluted and disappeared up the steps.

Cuthbert turned his attention back to me. I didn't like the look in his eyes. The guy was really intending to shoot me.

"What I don't understand," I said. "Is why you'd risk exposing this operation by kidnapping the wife of a well-known journalist."

His face tightened. For a second I thought he was going to pull the trigger.

"He did it to keep me from telling the world about his little operation," Leana said.

Cuthbert made a sound, a cross between a growl and a groan. "Nosy bitch's been nothing but trouble for me since the first time I got in a car she was driving. I should have killed you at Fort Belvoir."

"You bastard, you did the next best thing," she spat at him. "You destroyed my reputation."

I moved with my back almost touching the crates on my right, turning so I could see both of them. Cuthbert's attention was on Leana, but he was still too far away for me to risk making a move. While I watched the back and forth between them, I quickly scanned my surroundings for possible weapons to use against him. The pickings were slim, depending upon your point of view. From my point of view, with him holding a gun and me grabbing at air, they were pretty slim.

There was my K-bar knife, but I'd have to open my shirt and remove it from my belt, all movements that would take time and would be hard to accomplish before Cuthbert could squeeze the trigger. There was Lindsey's knife. On the floor, a few feet from Lindsey's outstretched hands where he'd dropped it when I broke his arm; it was blocked from

Cuthbert's view by Lindsey's body. There was, of course, Lindsey himself. Yeah, I was that desperate. I had no idea how I would use the unconscious man's body against his boss, but at that moment I wasn't discarding any possibilities. There were tons of them, literally tons I reckoned. Crates and crates of some pretty deadly weaponry. And, while I don't own a gun, don't carry a gun, and have only used a gun once since leaving the army, if it's a matter of me or the other guy, I'm willing to use whatever I can get my hands on. Therein, of course, lay the problem with Cuthbert's arsenal. By the time I could get one of the crates open, extract a weapon, unwrap it, load it, and point it at him, he would have emptied the M9's clip into my body. No, not one of my best ideas, I'll admit, but I was getting desperate.

In the meantime, their argument was escalating.

"It's about time you told me who else knows about this, Leana," Cuthbert said. "It'll make things go a whole lot easier."

"You mean it'll make it easier for you after you kill me? No thanks, I'll pass on that."

She was even tougher than I thought, and smart too. Even though I didn't have the details, I'd already concluded that the only thing keeping her alive was that she had some information Cuthbert wanted— needed—and, once he had it he no longer needed her. I could see it, too, in the frustration on his face.

"Look, it doesn't have to be like that," he said. "I can pay you, hey? Make up for the smear job we did on you. You could be rich beyond your wildest dreams."

"You're a bit late with that offer. Now, back in the day, when I was living on a staff sergeant's pay, I might—might—have been tempted. But, you forget, I'm now married to a famous writer. Believe it or not, writing about wine is quite lucrative. Jacob's written several books on the subject, and the royalties from them alone keep me quite comfortable." She laughed. "So, colonel, take your offer and stick it where the sun don't shine."

"Well, if you won't take my money, I guess I'll have to just get your cooperation another way, and I can assure you, you're not gonna like my methods . . . or the methods Ken . . . and Rob here, when he wakes up, will use to get that cooperation." He turned his attention to me. "As for you, Mr. Hotshot private eye, I think Rob's gonna have something special in mind for you when he wakes up."

"I hope it doesn't involve shooting," I said. I waved my arms around. "One stray round hits a crate of grenades, and you're gonna have an awful big hole in the ground." I chuckled. "Of course, there won't be enough of you left to give a damn."

His eyes narrowed as he followed the motion of my hand. "I wouldn't worry about that, Rob's not that fond of using guns. He's something of a cut up." He laughed at his own lame joke.

"Yeah, I noticed that when I came in. He likes cutting on women, does he? We'll have to discuss that when he wakes up. Of course, I don't think he'll be waking up for a while. Afraid I hit him a little harder than I intended."

"For a man who's about to die, you're a pretty cool character," he said. "We'll see how cool you are when Rob starts working on you."

"Hey, since you plan to kill me anyway, you mind telling me what all this shit's for? I mean, you got enough stuff here to supply a small army."

"Hell, I don't guess it matters much. Neither of you are gonna be telling anyone . . . else." He glared down at Leana. "Besides whoever you've told about it, that is."

"How do you know I haven't told the authorities?" she asked, giving him a defiant return glare.

"Try again, sweet cheeks. If you'd told anyone in authority, this place would be crawling with military cops and ATF. No, I'm worried you might have let it slip to someone else. I thought at first you might've told your husband, but after the way you two interacted, I decided probably not. Of course, there's always that lovely younger sister of yours."

Her face paled. "Y-you leave Laura out of this, you bastard. She doesn't know anything."

"I can vouch for that," I said.

"How can you do that?" she asked. "And, by the way, I know your name, and you obviously know mine, but how did you get mixed up in this?"

"The local authorities weren't getting anywhere, so your husband hired me to find you."

"Jacob is such a dear. I'm sorry I was so snippy with him. But, I wanted to check things out for myself, and I didn't want to get him involved."

"I'm sorry to break up this touching scene," Cuthbert said. "But, I've got a business to run and partners to keep satisfied." Lindsey's leg twitched, and Cuthbert smiled. "Looks like you miscalculated, Pennyback. Rob's about to come around; so you don't have much longer. You still want to know what's going on here?"

I eased back until my back was resting against the larger crate of MAAWS and draped my arm across the top of the crate of grenades.

"He'll still be a few minutes coming fully around, and a few after that until his head clears; so, yeah, I'd like to know what's going on. Why would a colonel betray his oath of office like this?"

"Hell, you can only go so far on a colonel's

pay, especially when you retire and they cut it in half. Let's just say I met some men who handle big, and I mean big, money. They made me an offer I couldn't refuse."

"You mean that slime ball, Maleky Barichnyev, the guy I saw giving you an envelope full of money?" Leana said.

"You weren't supposed to see that. If you'd stayed with your vehicle like you're supposed to, we wouldn't be here now."

"It's not my fault I had to go to the little girl's room. You two should've held your little tete a tete somewhere else."

"So," I said. "That's why you were hounded out of the army?"

"Yeah. This turd and his lap dogs started spreading rumors that I was shagging some of my VIP riders, and using drugs . . . and who knows what else. They even got a couple of light colonels to swear that I'd propositioned them. I'd planned to report what I saw, but by then it would've looked like I was trying to get revenge, so I just quit."

"Why did you come here, then?"

"When Jacob showed me the invitation and I saw Cuthbert's name, I wanted to come and see if it was the same person. I came, I saw, and it is the same ass hole. Unfortunately, Lindsey here recognized me. He and the other one, Adams, grabbed me before I could get back to the room and hauled me down here. I've been here ever since. Jacob must be worried sick."

My respect for this woman was going up by the second. Here she was, held against her will and obviously ill-treated, and she worried about her husband.

"He'll be happy to know you're okay," I said. "Just in case you didn't know it, he really cares a lot for you, too."

She smiled. Cuthbert snorted.

"Sorry to disappoint you, friend, but he's never gonna know she's okay. As soon as I find out who she might've talked to, she's gonna disappear."

I was getting tired of Cuthbert's voice, and his arrogance. But, I didn't let it show on my face. I looked at Lindsey out of the corner of my eye. His leg still twitched every few seconds, but he showed no signs of coming to. Cuthbert, his gun held loosely at his waist, had developed just the right amount of over confidence in his control of the situation. All that, though, could change rapidly. I had to make my move before Lindsey came around.

I looked at Leana and winked, and then cut my eyes toward Cuthbert. She smiled back.

"You know, Cuthbert," she said. "If you had any balls, you wouldn't send your tamed dogs down here to try and make me talk. Oh, I forgot, you don't have any balls. You know what your nickname was back at Fort Belvoir? Cuthbert the Cunt. Because you have no balls, you pencil dick motherfucker."

That got to him. His face went red, and his mouth twisted into an angry snarl. He raised the pistol and started toward her. "Why you dumb bitch, I'll—"

Before he could finish his sentence, I dropped my right arm into the space between crates and swept the crate of grenades toward him with as much force as I could manage. He'd leaned forward, so his head was in the direct line of flight of the box, which must have weighed ten or fifteen kilos. It caught him squarely on the ear, snapping his head to the side, and scraping a patch from his jaw. He raised his left hand to push at the box, yelling in pain. As the box bounced off his shoulder and he started turning and raising the pistol in his right hand, I grasped his wrist with my right hand, twisting and digging my thumb into the inside of his wrist, causing him to squeal and loosen his grip on the weapon. As he swept his left hand down to try and pry my hand from his wrist, I slammed him in the temple with my left fist, letting the knuckle of the second finger do the work. The blow stunned him, and he dropped the M9. I then hit his Adam's apple with a knife hand chop of my right hand. He made a gurgling sound and dropped to his knees, both hands going to his throat.

I knelt and picked up the M9, and pushed him over onto his back. He began to retch. I slipped the pistol into my belt, took out my

K-Bar and turned to cut the ropes binding Leana.

She sat there numbly for a few seconds while I massaged her wrists and ankles where the tight bindings had interfered with the blood flow.

She finally pushed my hands away and pushed herself up to a standing position, weaving a bit, but smiling like a trooper.

The door slammed open with a bang. Her mouth opened in an 'O,' and I whirled around to see Deputy Mansfield and a uniformed sheriff's deputy crouched with their weapons aimed at us.

"Get down on the floor and let me see your hands," he yelled.

I dropped the knife, went to my knees and clasped my hands on top of my head. Leana remained standing. "If you don't mind, officer," she said. "I've been sitting in this damn chair for almost two weeks. I think I'll remain standing."

TWENTY

"M-Mrs. Sonnenberg," Mansfield said, his eyes round like saucers. "You're alive."

"Well, that's kind of obvious now, isn't it," she said. "Although, if Mr. Pennyback hadn't come along when he did, I might not have been alive for very much longer."

That turned his attention back to me, and then to the two bodies sprawled on the floor.

"Pennyback, what the hell are you doing here?" he asked. "And, what's wrong with these two?"

Then, he looked around the room. The boxes and the words stenciled on them began to seep through to his overtaxed brain.

"What the holy hell is this place?"

"If you'll let me put my hands down and stand up, I'll tell you," I said.

He looked like he'd sucked on an unripe

lime. "Yeah, okay, get up," he said. "But, keep those hands where I can see 'em."

I slowly stood up, keeping my hands out from my sides.

"This, deputy, is one of the biggest arms smuggling rackets you're likely to ever bust in your entire career," I said. "And, for good measure, you've got the man who orchestrated the kidnapping of Leana Sonnenberg."

He looked from me to her with a question in his eyes.

"That's about it," she said. She pointed to Cuthbert, who was still massaging his throat and glaring daggers at me. "That man, Harlan Cuthbert, former Army Colonel Harlan Cuthbert, kidnapped me because when I was in the army I became aware of his connection to an arms dealer –"

"A Russian mobster by the name of Maleky Barichnyev," I completed her sentence for her. "Cuthbert's apparently been using this place as storage for weapons destined for Barichnyev." I was guessing on that, but I was willing to bet it was a damn good guess.

It got Mansfield's attention, though. "Holy shit," he said. "This guy's tied in with half the politicians in this county. He's been spreading money around like candy."

"Does that mean you're not going to arrest the son of a bitch?" Leana's voice was as cold as liquid nitrogen.

"No, ma'am," he said. "It just means there's gonna be a shit storm when I do." He smiled. "But, I'm gonna enjoy every minute of it." He turned to the uniformed officer. "Get someone in here and cuff these two and haul their asses up to a cruiser."

"There's another one," I said.

"Yeah, I know. Black guy was at the door with a rifle, but when he saw how many cops' guns were aimed at him, he saw the light and gave up. Tried to say he was looking for a prowler, but we cuffed him and put him in a cruiser anyway. Guess it was a good thing we did, huh?"

'Yes," I said. "I guess it was." I leaned down and picked up my K-Bar, and slipped it into the sheath strapped to my ankle. I picked up the switchblade, which the cops had overlooked when they hauled Lindsey out, handling it by the blade, I handed it to Mansfield.

As he took it gingerly, he frowned at me. I'd expected him to be at least a small bit happy that his case had been solved. He needed a little prodding.

"You know, your department's got a jump on ATF, the FBI, and just about everyone on this," I said. "You're likely to get national attention."

"Yeah, my partner will love that," he said. His look changed to that of a kid just swallowing a spoonful of castor oil. "She gets off on publicity. I just want to do my job and get home in one piece at night."

"I know what you mean." I grabbed the goggles from atop the crate and tucked them under my arm. "My partner, Heather, is the same way. Always bugging me to write my memoirs or give interviews to the press, when all I want to do is solve the case and move on."

His expression softened.

"Partners like that can be a real pain in the ass, can't they?"

Who would've thought that that would be the thing that allowed Mansfield and me to bond? I rolled my eyes.

"And, to make it worse, she always wants to get involved in all the action in the field. I mean, it's not as if she can't handle herself or anything, but I'd feel guilty if anything ever happened to her."

"Tell me about it." He copied my rolled eyes. "You'd think they'd appreciate that you're looking out for them, but no, they just complain. Christina's probably upstairs now bitching to the uniforms about how I left her up there to guard that perp Adams instead of bringing her down here where the real action is. Hah, some action this was."

"Gentlemen," Leana said. "You're talking as if we women can't handle ourselves, and that we *need* a big old man protecting us. Need I remind you that I held out against *three* big old men for nearly two weeks?"

Mansfield looked sheepish. I looked at her

and said, "There's no doubt that you're one tough person. I know my partner, Heather, is, and I'll bet Deputy Fontaine can hold her own in a fight."

"Well, damn right she can," Mansfield said. "I didn't mean to imply she couldn't. But, I'm from a generation that was taught that it was a man's duty to look after a woman." His cheeks turned red. "I guess it makes me act like a sexist ass hole sometimes."

"At least you're decent enough to admit it," she said. "Just let her know you respect her, and explain why you do the things you do. Hell, she probably already knows it, and just enjoys busting your chops."

He looked at me, his brows raised.

"I think she's probably right," I said. "I know my partner gets a thrill out of yanking my chain now and then."

Leana lifted an arm and sniffed at her arm pit. Her nose wrinkled and she frowned. "Now, if you two are finished with your kumbaya moment, I really need a long hot shower. I smell like . . . well, it would be unladylike of me to say."

"Don't you think you should get those bruises seen to first?" Mansfield said.

"Not until after I've washed the dirt and funky smell away. If you think I'm gonna take my clothes off for a doctor smelling like this, you have another think coming."

TWENTY-ONE

Leana made Mansfield and his partner wait until she'd showered, shampooed, and changed out of her dirty attire. I took advantage of the delay to get to know the two cops, and to fill them in on what I'd figured out and how. I gave them everything I could recall about the stockpile of weaponry, and the implications of such hardware getting into the wrong hands.

Mansfield took notes as I spoke, stopping now and then to blow out a gust of air and shake his head.

Fontaine showed a lot of interest in my night vision goggle, but tried to keep me from noticing. "How did you tumble to the fact that they were holding her here?" she asked. "Or that she wasn't dead and in a shallow grave somewhere?"

"Well," I said. "It was just a gut feeling at first, but one shaped by years of experience— and, not just as a private investigator. I was in the army for two decades. Unless you've got a good organization behind you, like the mob, and control over the environment, outside hectic combat, it's not all that easy to conceal a body . . . hell, it's not *that* easy in a war zone. Most of our missing in action are missing because their comrades had to leave them where they fell, and in the heat of combat and fog of war couldn't get back to retrieve them. This place is a lot like a chaotic battlefield; crawling with guests and staff, so burying someone on the grounds isn't really all that feasible, and there's a lot of risk of being seen if you try to move a body. Same thing goes for hanging onto one. After a day, a dead body starts to smell pretty ripe. It'd be hard to conceal the stench." I shrugged. It all sounded so pat after the fact, but that's the way it is. Retrospectives are always the models of clarity and precision.

She nodded. "Makes sense, but they could've killed her and buried her in that basement they were holding her in."

"I had no idea there was a basement until I entered tonight. Of course, that was always a possibility, but there'd still be the problem of getting rid of the dirt." I shrugged. "Like I said, it was just a gut feeling. Of course, there were some facts that supported it; like the fact that Cuthbert and Leana, Ms. Sonnenberg, both served in the army, and both were at Fort Belvoir at the same time. Did you know that she left the army suddenly right before she was up for officer training?"

They both shook their heads. "It never occurred to us," Mansfield said. "And, I have to confess, we never looked at Mr. Cuthbert as a suspect. I mean, with his political connections in the county and all, it just never crossed our minds that he'd be involved in something like . . . this."

"We screwed it on this one," Fontaine said.

"Don't be so hard on yourselves. When you're that close to an investigation, it's easy to overlook things," I said. "That's why having an outside eye look at things can be so valuable. I didn't have a stake in this other than delivering for my client. Hell, even I missed that hatch door the first time I was in that building. It didn't occur to me until later, which is why I put the place under surveillance."

"Yeah," Fontaine said, and her eyes now fixated on the goggles at my side on the sofa. "And in almost total darkness too. Where'd a private eye get gear like that? It must cost a bundle."

"I imagine it does, but I have it on loan from a friend of mine who has access to such goodies."

"Shit, the ones we have weigh a ton, and they're so damn bulky you can hardly move. What do these things weigh?"

"A pound or so," I said.

"And, it lets you see things clearly?"

I picked it up and put it on, but left the monocular up. "Yeah, and it has the advantage of leaving one eye free so you don't get blinded accidentally if a light comes on."

"Wow," she said. "What we could do with a piece of equipment like that. It'd change the game on night stakeouts. Say, you couldn't maybe, you know, misplace that thing, could you?"

I laughed. Since September 11, 2001, the military had, with congressional approval, been providing some civilian police forces with excess military equipment; everything from special armored vests to armored vehicles, but I didn't think the people in Blood's former agency were in on that little gift-giving scheme, or that they'd appreciate me for letting their little toy get out into the public.

"Sorry, but this model's not yet available outside of special channels."

"So, how'd you get your hands on it? Who could we talk to about getting a few?" Mansfield asked, looking at me with new respect.

Even Fontaine was regarding me with an expression that was no longer hostile.

"Like I said, I have a friend who has access. This is a prototype, not yet available for . . . distritubion." That was probably more than he needed to know, but he wasn't getting any more from me.

He knew it, too. He just smiled that little half smile that's almost a grimace.

"Can't kill a man for asking," he said.

Actually, I wasn't sure that was right. What I know about the secret intelligence agencies outside the military wouldn't impress a fifth grader, but I knew that Blood hadn't gotten his nickname from leading Cub Scouts. I decided to drop the subject.

Thankfully, while I sat there trying to think of something to say to divert their attention, Leana came into the little conference room that Paul Cobane had provided us.

She was a changed woman. She'd changed from her dirty and rumpled clothes into a blue skirt and green blouse that one of the hotel waitresses loaned. She still had the shiner and the bruise on her cheek, but she'd showered and shampooed, and her skin glistened from the water. I had no idea how the woman who'd loaned her the outfit looked in it, but Leana Sonnenberg filled it out to perfection.

Fontaine gave her one of those looks women give when another woman who makes other women look like chambermaids enters the room, while Mansfield just stared; his Adam's apple bobbing up and down.

Leana, though, was all poise. If it hadn't been for her black eye, I would never have guessed that she'd just been rescued from several days of imprisonment and mistreatment.

"Well," she said. "I'm ready to make my statement now, and then I just want to go home and sleep for the next few days."

Fontaine took a notebook and a small portable recorder from her bag, and Mansfield scrambled to get Leana a chair. I was a fifth wheel for the next thirty minutes as they walked her through everything that happened from the minute she and her husband got out of his car at the inn until the county sheriffs' deputies arrived.

She explained about accidentally seeing Cuthbert, when he was still an active duty colonel, receiving a thick envelope from a 'foreign' looking man at a reception hosted by a well-known defense contractor in Alexandria, Virginia. She'd at first thought nothing of it, but Cuthbert spotted her, and his and the foreigner's reactions had told her that she'd seem something she wasn't supposed to see. Her plan had been to report what she'd seen to her supervisor as soon as she returned to Fort Belvoir, but Cuthbert had beaten her back and started the rumors about her that basically ruined her career. She'd put the incident behind her until her husband announced that he'd been assigned by his magazine to visit Brandywine Estates and do a review of the vineyard's offerings. When she'd heard the name of the owner of the place, it all came back to her, and she'd insisted on accompanying him, to his surprise. Her intention had been to verify that the Brandywine Cuthbert was the same colonel she'd known in the army, and if he was, she'd decide what to do.

Unfortunately for her, Lindsey, who had been left to keep the tour group company had recognized her as soon as she recognized him as one of the soldiers from her time at Fort Belvoir. She'd made an excuse and headed back to the inn, deciding to go by way of the garden, but apparently Lindsey had alerted Cuthbert, and he'd sent him and Adams to snatch her. They'd wrapped her up in an old tarp and spirited her by way of the back service road to the wine press building, where Cuthbert had ordered them to do whatever was necessary to find out if she'd told anyone else about him.

She was no slacker, not this woman. I could see why she'd been considered officer material. She was tough, and she was smart, and even in a stressful situation, she'd kept her cool. Between sessions of 'questioning' at the hands of Lindsey and Adams, she'd taken in her surroundings, and realized that Cuthbert was involved in a massive arms smuggling operation, and from snippets of conversation between him and his henchmen, and ascertained that he was in the pockets of the Russian mob. Realizing that this was bigger than her kidnapping, she'd resolved to survive, and had resisted everything they'd done to her—and, her description of the physical abuse, sensory deprivation, and squalid conditions under which she'd been held, left Mansfield and

Fontaine looking grim and angry at the same time.

When she finished, Fontaine, her hand shaking, turned the recorder off.

"Ms. Sonnenberg," she said. "We'll get this statement transcribed, and I'll personally bring it to your home for your signature."

"Ah, speaking of that, how am I going to get home? Leana asked.

"We'll have a deputy drive you home," Mansfield said.

"If you don't mind waiting until I can retrieve my car, I'd be happy to give you a ride," I said. "That is, if it's okay with you two deputies?"

Mansfield shrugged and nodded his okay. Fontaine, her eyes still hungrily on my goggles, also nodded.

"We'll stay here with her until you get back," she said. "You want me to hold those goggles for you?"

"Good try, deputy," I said. "But, I wouldn't want you . . . accidentally misplacing them. Besides, they're not heavy. I've humped the boonies with a lot more than this."

"Give it a rest, Christina, that outfit's way out of our league," Mansfield said. "Man, you better get that thing out of here before she figures a way to relieve you of it."

He laughed. She punched his shoulder. I laughed. Leana looked confused. We bonded.

TWENTY-TWO

It took me thirty minutes to walk to my car, get the NVG stowed away out of Fontaine's sight, and drive back to the inn. I decided that the field workers could just clean up my bottles and food wrappers when they tended the vineyard. One visit there was enough for me, and it wasn't as if Cuthbert would be able to lodge a littering complaint against me.

Things had quieted down considerably by the time I got back. All the police vehicles were gone except for Mansfield and Fontaine's personal cars. It was 4:40 in the morning and the sky was beginning to turn a light gray. A murder of crows painted a series of dark marks against the bright sky as they circled the vineyard looking for food. They 'cawed' loudly as they circled. Leana, Mansfield and Fontaine were waiting for me on the verandah. Paul Cobane stood behind them, rubbing his hands together and shifting constantly from one foot to the other. His face was a study in conflicting emotions.

"What will become of the inn?" I heard him say as I mounted the steps. "What about the vineyards, the staff?"

"I guess it's yours to run until the legal issues are settled," Mansfield said.

Cobane's eyes lit up and he rubbed his hands together. The emotion that was clear on his face now was eager anticipation. I imagined he was already thinking about the changes he'd be making to *his* new empire, provided the government didn't seize it after Cuthbert was convicted, and with a basement space full of evidence supported by statements from Leana and me, his conviction was pretty much a sure thing.

I held the door for Leana and she got into my Volkswagen. The three on the verandah waved as I got in, put it in gear and drove away. They were still standing there when we went around the first turn in the road and the buildings disappeared behind the towering rows of vines.

The drive back into Washington took nearly two hours. Our departure from Brandywine had, unfortunately, coincided with the inbound commuter traffic. We rode in silence. After what Leana had been through, I felt she deserved the down time to process it.

It was 7:10 when I pulled into the driveway of the Sonnenberg house. The place looked quiet. A single light was on over the front door.

"You think your husband will be awake?" I asked.

"Yes, he's an early riser. He's probably in his study working on an article for the magazine."

He wasn't. He'd obviously been sitting in the living room and had heard my car. The door swung open as we approached. Jacob Sonnenberg, wearing a satin dressing gown, his bare feet encased in wool slippers, stood in the door with tears streaming down his cheeks.

Leana rushed forward and fell into his arms, and they cried together for a few seconds. She wrapped her arms around him, and he clung to her like a man grasping a life preserver.

"Oh, Leana, my love," he said in a choked voice. "I . . . I was so worried. I was afraid I'd never see you again."

She pulled back and wiped the tears from her cheeks. Then, she reached up and brushed his cheeks. "Jacob, darling," she said. "Don't you have any faith in me? You know I'd never leave you. Who'd be around to take care of you if I wasn't here?"

"I guess I'd have to do it," a soft, feminine voice said from the shadows in the doorway. Laura Colman, wearing faded jeans and a wrinkled gray sweatshirt, stepped into the halo of light from the fixture over the door.

"Laura, oh Laura, you're here," Leana said, pulling away and grabbing her sister in a bear hug.

"Of course I'm here, big sister. Someone had to take care of things for you while you were away. This husband of yours is useless around the house."

Releasing her sister, Leana looked from her to her husband. "Does this mean—"

"It means I was wrong to be angry with Jacob for taking you away from me," Laura said. "While you were missing, and after I talked with Mr. Pennyback here, I had time to think about how childish I was being, so I called Jacob to apologize."

"There was really no need for that," Sonnenberg said. "I should have been more sensitive to how you felt. I was the one who should have had the good sense to call you and apologize, but fortunately, good sense seems to run in the Colman family."

The two smiled at each other.

"Anyway," Laura said. "We came to the conclusion that we both love you, and decided that there's more than enough of you to go around."

Leana grabbed her sister's arm gently, and turned to Jacob, laying a hand on his forearm. "So, that means you two are finally friends?"

"No, it means we're family," he said. "It's

what we should have been from the beginning if I hadn't been so oblivious to other people's feelings."

"Better late than never, bro," Laura said.

I felt like I was intruding on a precious family moment. I turned to walk away.

"Wait, Mr. Pennyback," Sonnenberg said. "You can't leave until we've properly thanked you for bringing our Leana back."

"Oh yes, Mr. Pennyback," Leana echoed. "I've not yet properly thanked you for rescuing me." She turned back to the other two. "You should have seen him, like an avenging angel, he swooped down into that basement where they were holding me and beat them senseless, and they were armed. It was absolutely freaking amazing."

"I'm not sure that describes events accurately . . . well, except for the beat them senseless part."

Everyone except me laughed, but there was tension in the laughter. That, though, was to be expected. They, all three of them, had been through a lot. I followed them inside. I expected to stop in the sunken living room, but Laura, leading the way, kept on going toward the kitchen. As we approached it, the smell of bacon and freshly-brewed coffee filled the air. As tired and sleepy as I was from being up all night, my stomach started growling. At that moment I was at the bottom tier of Maslow's hierarchy of needs, the *grundbedurfnisse,* the physiological needs for food, drink, and rest—in that order.

In the kitchen, there was a plate on the counter near the stove with four slices of bacon on it. A skillet, still smoking, sat on the stove. The coffee maker on the counter was filled with dark brown liquid.

Leana looked at her husband with raised eyebrows and a look of wonder.

"Don't look at me," he said. "Laura did the cooking."

"He let me stay in your guest room last night. It was the least I could do."

"I was feeling pretty down when she called, so when she said she wanted to apologize, I . . . I invited her to come here and do it in person.'

Leana kissed him, and then kissed her sister.

"I'm so glad you two finally got together."

I just stood there breathing deeply, sucking in the aroma of coffee and bacon.

"That smells good," I said.

"I imagine you're hungry," Leana said. "You were up all night, and all that effort subduing those two thugs."

I looked at my watch. Sandra was probably already heading out the door for school, and if I went home, I'd only have to cook for myself. If I ate here, I'd be able to go home, shower and hit the rack.

"Yeah," I said. "I could eat an elephant right now."

"Well, just sit down and have some coffee

while I whip up something for all of us," Laura said.

While Laura broke eggs in a bowl and began scrambling them, Leana poured four cups of coffee. She put one on the counter near Laura and the rest on the small breakfast table. I took a sip. It was the same as I'd had when I visited Sonnenberg previously, but I was so hungry I paid no mind. I watched with interest as Laura chopped green onions, chili peppers and a couple of garlics, which she mixed into the beaten eggs. She then put chunks of provolone cheese and three tablespoons of milk in the mixture, mixed it up and poured it into the skillet which she'd put back on the burner. In a matter of minutes, she was using a spatula to ladle a mound of fluffy yellow scrambled eggs onto a large platter. She then toasted eight slices of whole wheat bread. She put mounds of eggs, two pieces of toast, and a slice of bacon on four plates and put them on the table.

We ate in silence. It was good, as good as I could do. My plate was clean in minutes.

"You have quite an appetite, Mr. Pennyback," she said. "Would you like more?"

"No, I'm good, and please, after feeding me a meal like that, you have to call me Al."

"Okay, Al," she said, fluttering her lashes and smiling at me. "I'd be happy to do breakfast for you anytime you like."

"I appreciate that, but right now, I need to call my girlfriend, Sandra, and let her know I'm on my way home."

She looked disappointed. "Oh well, my loss."

"Look, folks, I've really got to run," I said. "Ms. Sonnenberg, Leana, I'm happy you're okay and home. You're a strong woman, but you were in the army, you know that a trauma like this can come back to haunt you. I was in the army, so I know the drill. If you find yourself needing someone to talk to, give me a call. Your husband has my number." She was strong, but post-traumatic stress is a bitch. You can go years after an incident without a problem, and then it hits you like an out-of-control locomotive. The look on her face told me that she understood that.

"Thanks, Al. I'll keep that in mind."

Outside, after getting in my car, I decided to give Sandra a call. She deserved to know I was okay and back in town. I took out my phone and dialed her mobile number, hoping I wouldn't be interrupting her in the middle of a class.

She answered on the first ring. "Al, are you okay? You're not calling while driving are you? You know that's not safe, and it's against the law in Maryland. How long before you get home?" The words came tumbling out of her. I could hear the tension in her voice.

"I'm okay, babe. I'm parked, and I'll be at the house in about half an hour. I should be rested by the time you get home from school."

"I'm not at school, babe. Have you forgotten; it's Saturday. I'll be here when you got home. You're okay, right?"

I had lost track of the time. "I'm fine, really fine. Oh, and Leana Sonnenberg was recovered safely. The bad guys are all behind bars."

"Well, Al Pennyback, you get your ass home as quickly as you can. I have a surprise for you when you wake up, and after that you can tell me all about your little adventure."

Charles Ray

TWENTY-THREE

Sandra kept her word. After I got home, and after she hugged and kissed me until I begged her to let me come up for air, she allowed me to shower and go to bed alone to sleep until late in the afternoon. She shook me awake at 5:30, and gave me her surprise, and then we lay cuddled in each other's arms until nearly 7:00 when we finally got up and fixed supper. While we were eating I told her what happened, leaving nothing out. She didn't say anything, but after I'd finished my story, she got up, came around the table and sat in my lap with her arms around my neck and her forehead resting against mine.

It went that way the whole weekend. I took one break on Sunday morning to call Heather and give her a brief summary, with a promise to give her a full briefing for our case file on Monday morning, and then afterwards we drove to Blood's house to return the night vision goggles. While Elizabeth and Sandra sat in the living room and chatted, he and I sat on the front porch and I gave him a detailed review of their performance. Afterwards, we had lunch together around the rough wood table in the living room and were back home by mid-afternoon.

Sandra tried to put on a brave face, especially when I told her about confronting Cuthbert in the cellar room where Leana was being held, but I noticed that the only time she let me out of her sight the whole rest of the weekend was when I had to go to the crapper, and I was pretty sure she lurked somewhere near the bathroom door at those times.

She was better by Monday morning and completely over it by the middle of the week, especially after NPR news announced the indictment in Fauquier County of a 'notorious' gang of kidnappers, and the uncovering of an international arms smuggling operation by the Fauquier County Sheriff's Department. I was surprised that the FBI and ATF had let the local cops get the public glory. I was pretty sure, though, that Mansfield and Fontaine were walking on air when that news story hit. Other than a cryptic statement that 'local authorities were assisted in their investigation by an unnamed civilian investigator,' no mention was made of yours truly. That didn't go over too well with Heather. She thought that the publicity would have been good for our business. I didn't care. The people who count, mainly Quincy, Buster, my friends, and the law enforcement authorities with whom I have to maintain a kind of détente, knew that I'd been the one to break the case. The people who drift in for our help from the street don't listen to NPR, and only read the sports and comic sections of the paper—and, on occasion the style section—so, I didn't see anything to be gained other than the possibility of being harassed by reporters wanting to get the nitty gritty about the case, which I wouldn't be able to share with them anyway. Sandra was happy that I wasn't mentioned in the news, which helped smooth things over on the home front a lot.

On Friday of that week, just before I set out for work, an obscure news item on NPR caught my attention.

"Federal authorities report arresting a Russian crime figure suspected of providing illegal arms to domestic extremist groups and international terrorists," the news anchor on 'All Things Considered' said. The radio news reporters didn't know much, but what they did know explained why the FBI and ATF had been willing to allow Fauquier County to hog the glory on Cuthbert's arrest. They'd been going after much bigger fish.

After arriving at the office and learning that Heather didn't know any more than what I'd heard on the radio, I called Buster to see if he'd picked up anything from his fed contacts. Luckily he had. I called Heather into my office and put the phone on speaker so she could get the information first hand.

"The junk that Cuthbert dude had in the cellar was just the tip of the iceberg," Buster said. "When his two thugs started dropping a dime on him and the cops laid out the evidence they had on him, he decided to flip on his bosses. When he did that, the feds were creaming in their jeans over what came out of his mouth."

It turned out that Maleky Barichnyev was just the U.S.-based boss of the Russian operation. Cuthbert had met Barichnyev's boss, Viktor Mashnikov, a former GRU colonel who had traded his uniform for the padded-shoulder, wide-collar suits of a mob boss when the Soviet Union collpased. The FBI had nabbed Barichnyev just as he was about to board an Amsterdam-bound KLM flight at JFK. Seems he'd seen the news reports of Cuthbert's arrest and rightly guessed his American stooge would rat on him. Unfortunately, the Russian had nearly a million dollars stashed in secret compartments of his luggage—unfortunately for him, a great find for the feds—so, realizing that he was caught red-handed, and in exchange for a guarantee that he'd be placed in some kind of protective detention, he ratted his own boss out. The phone lines between Washington and Brussels were superheated with the information flowing back and forth, and the Europeans, with Interpol coordinating operations, were salivating at the opportunity to give the Russian gangsters infecting western Europe bloody noses.

"I guess everyone's pretty happy," I said.

"Not exactly, bro. Between Cuthbert and Barichnyev, the feds have a list of organizations that they shipped weapons to that's as long as my arm. They got white supremacist groups and militias here in the states and a couple of al Qaeda wannabe groups setting up in Europe. They even sold guns to some neo-Nazi group in Germany. ATF's already made some arrests here, the French rolled up a terror cell that was just about to launch an attack, and the Germans did a number on the skinheads. I reckon there are some dudes pretty pissed right now on both sides of the pond."

"I guess they would be," I said. "They probably paid a princely sum for the weapons, only to get them confiscated."

"With some hard time in jail to boot for some of their top guys. Same thing in Europe. You know, Cuthbert and Barichnyev will be lucky if they manage to do a year of the time they'll get," he said.

"You mean they'll make some kind of a deal to get lighter sentences?" Heather asked.

"No, baby doll, because someone's gonna stick a shiv in them first time the guards aren't looking. You don't screw with these Aryan Brotherhood dudes. They got members in nearly every prison in the country. Any of the Russians that get convicted in Europe are likely to get the same treatment, plus the terrorists that didn't get rolled up are gonna be looking for 'em, and I wouldn't want to be in their shoes if they ever catch 'em."

She looked sad. I couldn't really feel sorry for either of them, though. They'd provided guns to people who'd planned to use them to hurt a lot of innocent people. As far as I was concerned, they deserved what they got, they all did. I didn't say it aloud, though. Heather already thought me a little barbaric because I insisted on meat with my meals. I saw no point in confirming that, in fact, I'm more than just a *little* barbaric. I'm not in favor of the death penalty, mind you. Too much chance of a wrong conviction, with no way to say 'sorry,' after the execution. But, if the bad guys want to do each other in, I say 'go for it,' and shed no tears.

"Well, everything worked out as far as we're concerned," I said. "I got my client's wife back safe, and got a pretty good fee in the process."

"Not to mention coming to the attention of one of the area's most famous journalists," Heather added.

"Yeah, that too, except I read one of the articles he wrote, and I didn't understand a word of it."

She made a sucking-sour-lemons face. "That's because you have no class, partner."

"You tell 'im, baby doll," Buster said. He laughed. "I been tryin' to tell him for years he needs to get some class."

"Oh, be quiet, Buster Mayweather," she said. "You're as bad as he is."

Laughing, he hung up.

"See what I mean," she said. "A gentleman wouldn't have hung up like that."

"Tell you what, why don't we take the rest of the week off, kiddo?"

She gave me a funny look. "It's not April First, Al. Can we really afford taking time off?"

"Look around you, Heather," I said, waving my arms around. "Do you see clients lining up at the door? No. Besides, the fee we got from Sonnenberg will cover us for the next two months. You did a great job backing me up, and you worked real hard on this case. You deserve it."

"You mean, you want to take a long weekend, is what you mean." She was turning and heading for the door as she spoke. "Okay, go ahead. I have some cleaning to do at home anyway," she said over her shoulder.

I wasn't too far behind her. She was shutting her computer down as I breezed through the door.

Charles Ray

TWENTY-FOUR

Saturday morning was perfect. The air was crisp and the sky was a clear blue with just the slightest wisps of clouds. We hardly worked up a sweat on our morning run, but made up for it in the barn working on the heavy bag afterwards. Sandra insisted on a little martial arts sparring after the heavy bag, which almost did me in. The woman's tireless—and competitive as hell. I had to pull every trick I'd learned working with my sensei in Korea to keep her from kicking my butt, and even with the tricks she got in a couple of good shots, including a sweeping kick that knocked my legs from under me and put me flat on my back.

That was it for me. "I yield," I said. "You're the winner today."

I stood and bowed to her. She returned the bow, but the Cheshire cat grin on her face would have mortified my instructors, in both taekwondo and kung fu, who had always taught me never to gloat or take pride in defeating an opponent. On the way back to the house, I insisted that she join me in meditating before we showered.

"I really need to shower," she protested. "I smell like sweaty gym socks."

"You need to clean your mind and spirit before your body," I said. I guided her to the porch and, sternly gave her directions with my eyes to assume a sitting position.

She complied, drawing her legs into a perfect Lotus position, something my banged up legs will not allow me to do. She understood the importance of meditation, and, while she was not as rigorous about doing it every day as I was, when she did, she put herself fully into it. I didn't have to be looking at her to know when the grin left her face to be replaced by an expression of peaceful repose. That also was something I'd learned from the men who'd taught me the martial arts. If you make a mistake, do not dwell on it. Realize it, correct it, and move on. Meditation helps you achieve that kind of balance. Sandra was a quick study who'd learned that on her own.

After twenty minutes, I took a deep breath and stood in one fluid motion. She followed me to a standing position, only more gracefully than I can manage.

"Thanks, babe," she said. "I feel so much better now. I'll feel perfect, though, when we've washed the funk off our bodies."

I bowed again. "Say no more, dear lady. I'll scrub your back.

"And, front too," she said, punching my arm, whirling, and dashing inside toward the bathroom.

I didn't chase after her. Instead, I took my time. Afterwards, in the shower, I took my time again. Sex is not quite as relaxing as meditation, but it runs a close second.

She was much more restrained as we prepared breakfast. The smile was there, but it was from the aroma of sausages and hash browns frying in pans on the stove and coffee merrily brewing in the pot on the counter rather than the thought of putting on my butt—or, at least, I hoped it was. While she tended the stovetop items, I mixed up a batch of biscuits, topping each with a square of American cheese before putting them in the oven. We stood at the counter and had coffee while the biscuits baked. When they were done, I cracked four eggs into a bowl, added chopped onions, pepper, garlic powder, chunks of cheese and half a cup of milk, and scrambled them in the skillet she'd used for the sausage.

"Say, why don't we have breakfast on the porch?" I said.

"Sounds like a good idea. You get the food, and I'll take the coffee and juice out and start setting up that travesty of a patio table you have out there."

I frowned at her jibe at the metal table I'd found at a yard sale. For two bucks, it was a steal, and had only required three hours with a box of steel wool to remove the rust. Of course, I'd removed most of the original yellow paint in the process, and had never gotten around to repainting it, but it was a good place to put the beer on those occasions when the weather was good and Buster could get a pass from Alma to come over on a weekend and have a few cold ones with me.

"Okay, okay, I promise, I'll go to Home Depot this afternoon and buy some paint," I said. "When I get done with that table, it'll look as good as new."

"I don't care about new," she said. "I'd just like it to look like it didn't just come from a junkyard. Now, start getting that food on plates, I'm starving."

"You shouldn't engage in hyperbolic speech, babe, not after meditating anyway."

She laughed. "Yeah, and you shouldn't engage in hyperbolic sounds from your midsection." She pointed at my gut.

The sounds were loud enough to hear from a foot away. "All right, you got me there. Get the coffee and juice, and while you're at it, pull out a bottle of that brandy. I think a dollop or two will make the coffee taste even better."

And, it did. After we'd finished eating, I poured each of us a second cup of Jamaican coffee, and then added a generous amount of brandy to each.

Lifting my cup, I touched it softly to hers, and then took a sip. The bittersweet taste of the brandy mixed well with the nuttiness of the coffee. I sat back and sighed. So did she.

After another sip, she put her cup down, reached over and took my cup from me and put it on the table. She then took my hand and held it there, resting on the table.

"Now," she said. "This is the way to spend a Saturday morning. Just sitting here, looking at the sky and trees, and letting the cool morning breeze wash over us."

I couldn't argue with that—wouldn't if I could. I knew a kind of peace with her that I'd not known in a long time.

"It doesn't get any better than this," I said.

She made a face at me. "Really? That's not what you said in the shower earlier."

"Uh, I mean here on the porch."

Now, her expression turned sultry. "Speaking of that, we have all the privacy in the world out here . . ."

Before I could respond to what was sounding like an invitation, two deer stepped out of the woods; a doe and a fawn. The fawn still had the white spots of an immature deer.

"Oh, look," she said. "A family of deer. Aren't they beautiful?"

They are beautiful creatures. Despite being carriers of Lyme disease that infects the ticks that cling to them. But, there was something else about this pair that caught my eye. Years of trekking through jungles, learning to spot the most subtle differences in my surroundings, I've developed a pretty accurate memory, and I was sure I'd seen these two before. Moreover, there was something about the way they walked, staying close to each other, and occasionally looking back into the trees. Then, it hit me. We'd seen them before. Only, the last time we'd seen them, there had been three.

The piebald fawn, the young male, was missing.

I felt a sad weight settling over me as I watched the doe stand vigil while the fawn stretched to suck at a teat. I would never know what had happened to the piebald. Brought down by a predator, hit by a car as they crossed a road, taken by a hunter for bragging rights, or just succumbed to the abnormalities that are common to that small percentage born piebald; whatever the reason, it was gone. A small piece of rare beauty as happens in nature sometimes. And, like many things, what nature gives, nature takes away. I considered sharing that with Sandra, but the look of wonder in her eyes as she watched the two deer held me back.

Reaching deep within myself, I sought that middle way, the path between ecstasy and despair. The answers to life's mysteries are always there. I felt bad about that beautiful, if somewhat misshapened baby deer. But then, I figure that by giving us ephemeral glimpses at beautiful things, Mother Nature is reminding us that nothing is permanent, and we ought to take full advantage of the beautiful things for the short time we have them.

Innocence is gone soon enough from this world. There's no sense ruining it for those who still possess it.

I grasped her hand, lifted it up, and kissed it.

"Yes, they are beautiful," I said.

Charles Ray

More adventures of Al Pennyback

Deadly Vendetta

When a bomb intended for a local mobster kills the wife of one of Al's old army buddies, and the law doesn't seem interested, it's up to Al and his friends to see that justice is done.

Death Wish

In the wake of the 9/11 terrorist attacks, there is a lot of money to be made in working for the government. There are some who will do anything to earn a profit, despite the best efforts at oversight. When a young sergeant who notices irregularities goes missing, his commander asks Al to find him.

A Deadly Wind Blows

Al is hired to find a missing heiress and convince her to return to Washington to claim her inheritance. Someone is determined to stop him, even if it means killing him.

See these and other books by this author at: http://www.amazon.com/Charles-Ray/e/B006WMLEZK

Charles Ray

Other books by this author:

Al Pennyback mysteries

Color Me Dead
Memorial to the Dead
Deadline
Dead, White, and Blue
A Good Day to Die
The Day the Music Died
Die, Sinner
Deadly Intentions
Death by Design
Till Death Do Us Part
Deadly Dose
Dead Man's Cove
Dead Men Don't Answer
Deadly Paradise
Kiss of Death
Death in White Satin
Death and Taxis
Deadbeat
A Deadly Wind Blows
Death Wish
Deadly Vendetta
A Time to Kill, A Time to Die
Dead Ringer
Death of Innocence

The Buffalo Soldier series
Buffalo Soldier: Trial by Fire
Buffalo Soldier: Homecoming
Buffalo Soldier: Incident at Cactus Junction
Buffalo Soldier: Peacekeepers
Buffalo Soldier: Renegade
Buffalo Soldier: Escort Duty
Buffalo Soldier: Battle at Dead Man's Gulch
Buffalo Soldier: Yosemite
Buffalo Soldier: Comanchero
Buffalo Soldier: Range War
Buffalo Soldier: Mob Justice
Buffalo Soldier: Chasing Ghosts

Ed Lazenby mysteries
Butterfly Effect
Coriolis Effect

Other fiction
Angel on His Shoulder
She's No Angel
Child of the Flame
Pip's Revenge
Wallace in Underland
Further Adventures of Wallace in Underland
Dead Letter and Other Tales
The White Dragons
The Dragon's Lair
Dragon Slayer

The Last Gunfighters
The Culling
Frontier Justice: Bass Reeves, Deputy
  U.S. Marshal
Angel on His Shoulder-Revised Edition
Battle at the Galactic Junkyard
Mountain Man
Devil's Lake

Nonfiction
Things I Learned from My Grandmother About
  Leadership and Life
Taking Charge: Effective Leadership for the
  Twenty-first Century
Grab the Brass Ring
African Places: A Photographic Journey
  Through Zimbabwe and southern Africa
A Portrait of Africa
There's Always a Plan B
In the Line of Fire: American Diplomats in
  the Trenches
Advice for the Insecure Writer
Looking at Life Through My Lens

Children's books
The Yak and the Yeti
Samantha and the Bully
Molly Learns to Share
Where is Teddy?
Catie and Mister Hop-Hop

Charles Ray

About the Author

Charles Ray has been writing fiction since his teens. He won a Sunday school magazine writing contest when he was thirteen, and having his byline on a short story published in a national publication forever hooked him on writing. During his time in the army (1962-1982) he often moonlighted as a newspaper or magazine journalist, and was the editorial cartoonist for the Spring Lake (NC) News, a weekly newspaper, during the 1970s. In addition to his writing, he was an artist/cartoonist and photographer for a number of publications, including Ebony, Eagle and Swan, and Essence, and had a monthly cartoon feature and did several covers for Buffalo, a now-defunct magazine that was dedicated to showcasing the contributions of African-Americans to the country's military history.

After retiring from the army, he joined the U.S. Foreign Service, and served as a diplomat in posts in Asia and Africa until his retirement in 2012. He has worked and traveled throughout the world (Antarctica is the only continent he hasn't visited), and now, as a full time writer, continues to globetrot looking for interesting things to write about, draw, or take pictures of.

A native of Texas, he now calls Maryland

home. For more on his writing and other projects, check one of the following Web sites:

http://charlesaray.blogspot.com
http://charlieray45.wordpress.com
http://www.twitter.com/charlieray45
http://www.facebook.com/charlieray45
http://www.flickr.com/photos/charlesray45/
http://www.viewbug.com/member/charlesray

www.ingramcontent.com/pod-product-compliance
Lightning Source LLC
Chambersburg PA
CBHW071458170626
46811CB00007B/2624